Mrs John Crawford

Songs of all Seasons, Climes and Times,

A Motley Jingle of Jumbled Rhymes

Mrs John Crawford

Songs of all Seasons, Climes and Times,
A Motley Jingle of Jumbled Rhymes

ISBN/EAN: 9783744773041

Printed in Europe, USA, Canada, Australia, Japan

Cover: Foto ©Andreas Hilbeck / pixelio.de

More available books at **www.hansebooks.com**

SONGS OF ALL SEASONS.

CLIMES AND TIMES.

A MOTLEY JINGLE OF JUMBLED RHYMES.

BY

MRS. JOHN CRAWFORD.

Toronto:

ROSE PUBLISHING COMPANY,

1890.

TO THE READER.

THERE are two things about a book which I always skip,—the preface and the moral. If the public are like me therein, I shall not feel grieved if they only read what comes between the two.

A preface is either an explanation or an excuse. If an explanation, it does for the book what explanation does for a joke,—takes the pith out of it. If an excuse, it shows that the writer considers an apology necessary. I cannot make an explanation of the contents of this little book, which I offer to the reader, for I don't see any need of it. It might be in better taste to offer an apology for placing such crude ideas before the public, but that, too, I forbear.

To those who read it, the book will be its own explanation and apology. And the book which does not convey its own meaning and moral, should neither be written nor read.

THE AUTHOR.

CONTENTS.

SONGS OF ALL SEASONS,

CLIMES AND TIMES.

L' ENVOI.

I SENT on the sea a ship one day,
  Laden with hope, love, and joy ;
Of all good wishes I made a crew,
  And the Captain, a beardless boy.

'Twas a silly venture of mine, they said,
  The greybeards who saw it go ;
But I cared for the counsel of none, not I!
  I feared not the face of woe.

I've waited and watched, this many a day,
  For my ship to return to me ;
But the white-winged bird of the deep glides on
  Over life's treacherous sea.

Will it ever return ? Ah ! the day was so bright,
  Earth fair, and the sky so blue,

When I saw my good ship from the shore glide
away
And lessen, then vanish from view.

I am told by those who are wiser than I,
That my ship and its cargo are gone;
But I still wait and watch, and hope for the day
When my Captain and crew will return!

THE BRETON MARINER'S PRAYER.

"Keep me, my God! My boat is so small and
Thy ocean is so wide!"

WHILE my tiny bark shall ride
O'er Thy ocean, deep and wide,
Keep me, my God! Let me be
Full of holy faith in Thee!

Ah! so small and weak my bark,
And Thy waves so cold and dark!
Heaving now in mighty wrath,
Now a smooth and shining path!

O'er Thy waves my small ship sails,
Grant, Great Captain, pleasant gales;
Still the tempests, howling wild,
Send me safe to wife and child.

Then, when darksome Death comes on,
Grant me, God, through Thy dear Son,
Safe to reach Thy port of peace,
Where all storms and sorrows cease!

A SONG OF THE SEA.

"O Poet, sing me a song of the sea,
Where my good ship glides gay and free;
Where my sailor sings in the snowy shrouds,
Heedless of storms or darkening clouds,
That cast on the waters a sombre hue,
Yet my vessel gaily dashes through.
Yet sing not of storms or scowling waves
That cover so many poor sailors' graves;
Make the picture bright, like the beaming ray
Which the sun's eye throws on this still, shut bay!"

"Ah, maiden! Let thy young life be
Afar from the world's great noisy sea!
Be always as now, fair, pure and gay,
Contented to dwell near thy little bay.
No wild winds wail o'er its surface small,
Thy tiny bark may go safe through all.
Think not of that vessel, bold and free,
That stems the storm of the wide, dark sea;
Think not of that sailor who climbs the mast,
Singing gay songs with no thought of the past.

"That vessel may sink at last, little maid!
It may go down when the storm is stayed,
Though it weather the gale, with each set sail
Untouched, unharmed by the wind's loud wail;
It may go down with no wave on the sea,
When sailor and storm sleep peacefully.
A strange, wild mystery is that wave,
Voiceful yet silent, mirthful yet grave;
All moods and changes are centred there,
Fickle and false, uncertain as air;

And the dwellers upon it are apt to be
Unstable and cold, like the briny sea.
Then let it sing its anthem grand,
And, little maiden, content thee on land.
Or, at most, let thy shallop at close of day
Find a port on the shore of this still, shut bay.
Choose thou a lover upon the shore,
Whom no storms of passion will e'er sweep o'er;
Live thou apart in this quiet vale,
Brave not thou, maiden, the world's rude gale."

"Ah! Poet, thou singest a saddening song!
I love a sailor—have loved him long.
Would'st thou assume that the sailor free
Partakes of the sea's inconstancy?
If so, then is the land lover cold,
Because he partakes of the earth's green mold.
All sink under great calamity,
Then why not my ship go down at sea?
When timbers are rotten and sails all torn,
Why drift o'er the sea a thing forlorn?
Nay! rather sink and proudly die
Than float to be scorned by the world's proud eye.
That my sailor is true has been tried and shown,
So are ever those who have danger known.
Only cowards live in inglorious ease,
Brave spirits breast many tumultuous seas.
This life is only a rolling sea
Far reaching out to eternity;
Some ships ride on the crest of the waves,
And their crews and captains seek gallant graves;
Some, lured by the shining yellow sand,
Ride near, till the gale drives them on the land.
Some cannot stand the sea's rude shock,
So, crouching, are dashed upon the rock.

Some little boats may sail on the bay,
But for me, let me ride in my ship away;
Away, far out on the deep, blue sea,
There only is safety, security!"

THE SAILOR'S WIFE.

BY-LOW, my baby, by-low-by!
Your father's ship 's at anchor nigh;
How gaily it rides on the glassy waves
That cover so many poor sailors' graves!
His heart is at anchor, his hopes are stayed
On his home and his precious little maid.
Sleep soft, my bird, within your nest,
Our hearts and our hopes with the ship at rest.

Be gay, my baby, brave and gay!
Your father's ship sails away to-day,
And he must not see a saddened face,
For that's to a sailor's wife disgrace.
The sea he loves, and the ship so trim,
But, oh, my baby, we'll pray for him,
That he may come back to us some day,
And so we will both be brave and gay.

By-low, my baby! Hush, my child!
Why start with terror, sudden, wild?
Hear'st thou the wind's loud, angry roar?
The breakers thundering on the shore?
O, wifely heart, oppressed with care,
Seek refuge now in God, in prayer!
Sleep sweet, my bird, while clouds droop low,
And requiem waves roll sad and slow.

Awake, my baby! Lift thy head
From off thy dainty, white-robed bed!
Thy father's safe, my nestling dear!
It is but joy that brings this tear;
His clasp is holding mother, child!
What care I though the waves roll wild?
Now slumber softly, sigh no more,
Our heart's wild storm of anguish o'er.

UNFINISHED.

THIS is a picture which we paint to-day,
In memory of one now passed away—
A youth of promise. See the sketch which gleams
From yonder wall—unfinished as it seems,
Yet like the hand that laid the pencil down,
Exchanging laurel wreath for heavenly crown.

* * *

A narrow strip of shining yellow sand
Loses itself in greenness on the land;
But, seaward looking, shines and simmers on
'Neath wanton waves, which, toying, float upon
And o'er it, and recede, and dimpling sparkle
'Neath the sun's rays, and then in denseness darkle
In secret recesses of caverns deep,
Where the sweet mermaiden doth lie asleep
Upon her couch of pearl, fringed with seaweed,
Regal in loveliness, a queen indeed,
And glittering with gems and jewels, rare
As the golden glittering of her long, bright hair,
That, lying thus, streams o'er her pearly pillow
In waves more shining than the sunlit billow.

How solemn and how still this summer eve!
No sail in sight, the harbor empty and bare
Save for the gulls that, screaming, wheel their flight,
Now sailing far aloft in the purpling air;
One diving down to where a venturous fish,
Leaping to catch its glittering evening meal,
Finds itself caught and borne along above
Its native element! See the others wheel
And still pursue their comrade, who still holds
The writhing fish, and flies; and at the last,
Hard pressed and weary, drops its prey again
Into the sparkling wave from whence it passed;
Then rising higher, but pursued no more,
Continues his calm flight along the shore.

The sun descending slow, leaves golden lines
On the still waves, which, as the last ray shines,
Deepen to darker tints, and seem to hold
The lake in trance, and like a sheet unrolled
Of rare mosaic set with precious gems—
Rich as are Oriental diadems,
In opal and in amethystine gleams.
To the east the mild, entrancing moon there beams,
Emerging from its mysterious bank of cloud,
That looms about it like a purple shroud.
It throws upon the waves beneath its feet
A slowly silvering path, and seems to greet
With gentle, loving smile, the retreating rays
Of the fond sun, on which it loves to gaze.

* * * * *

This seems the tale the artist's pencil told.
So far the sketch is perfect—but behold,
Upon the beach drawn up, the fisher's pride,
With spars and ropes half outlined. On its side

Lies the good boat, unfinished! Storm or shine
Can never matter to this craft of thine,
My boy, whose life was done ere manhood's day!
The stalwart youth just arming for life's fray,
Whose hopes, whose fears, whose aspirations broke
Away from earth as life to love awoke!
What higher knowledge, what divinest love
The life cut short on earth will find above!
Seeing and knowing only can we tell
The life we thought unfinished, ended well!

STANDING BY THE SHORE.

I STAND on the shore of an inland sea;
The airs of Autumn about me play;
The waves roll dark and heavily,
And the sun through clouds sheds a sickly ray.

Sadly I gaze on the frowning waves,
Dark as the hue of my hopes they roll;
O, that they floated above my grave
And shut out the day from my weary soul!

One lone ship sails steadily on,
Till below the verge she sinks from sight;
And her course she keeps till her port is won,
And the day finds rest in the arms of night.

But I? O God! What rest for me?
As I watch the ship in her onward track,
I remember that under the waves of this sea
Lies one whom I love,—and who comes not back!

He sailed away in the early light
Of a smiling morn in the month of June;
And the sun made the face of the waters bright
As they washed the beach with a low love tune!

He comes not back! and his vacant chair
Still stands in its old accustomed place;
The books that he loved are laid with care,
And there from the wall gleams his pictured face.

Well! Life is never quite what it seems;
Not I alone have this lesson learned;
And I rouse myself from my sad day-dreams,
With a sigh for "the ship that never returned."

"THE LASS THAT LOVES A SAILOR."

A LONG, level coast and a steel-blue sea,
And with white sails spread, a ship rides free;
A purplish mass overshadows the sky,
As the vessel gaily dashes by;
Gaily she rides o'er the swelling tides,
And glad sings the sailor as gently she glides;
Sing cheerily, sailor! Down by the sea
One whom thou lovest is watching for thee!
Folding her shawl to shield her slight form,
Praying that He send no wind, nor storm;
Crouching behind the sheltering rocks,
While the soughing surf her agony mocks.
Beating the shore like a living thing,
While far out the white gull dips its wing
In the crest of the wave, nor heeded not
That beneath him, where sunlight reacheth not,

Lie the mouldering bones of unfortunate ones.
To avert such fate the maiden moans,
While the sailor sings aloft in the shrouds,
Caring neither for storm nor darkening clouds.
Sing cheerily, sailor! A woman for thee
Watcheth and prayeth unceasingly!
Prayers from a pure heart will shield thee from harm,
No thought of danger e'er need thee alarm.
Sing cheerily, sailor! Down by the sea
Heaven send thee safe to her who waiteth for thee!

A DREAM-SHIP.

Sailing away,
Sailing away,
Over an ocean of sparkling spray;
White sails gleam,
And pennants stream,
From the spars of the ship that I see in my dream.

Sailing away,
Day after day;
Over the deep glides the ship so gay.
The sun shines bright
On its sails so white,
And the moon in its turn lights it up by night.

Cloudless blue skies
Above it rise,
And the sapphire sea beneath it lies;
While my good ship glides,
Both wind and tides
Seem made for its weal and naught besides.

CAZENOVIA LAKE.

DECEMBER IN 1866.

LIST to the low moaning lake close by,
Lying beneath the sombre sky;
Moaning and groaning and tossing in pain—
For the Ice-King is coming to regally reign.
Over the bosom once sparkling and bright
He spreadeth a strongly-made mantle of white;
He holdeth it firm in a warm clasp of love,
But he shutteth it out from the arched sky above;
So, repining, it moaneth in sorrow and pain,
Till the spring-time shall give it its freedom again.
The winter wind whistles my wide window by;
Gray clouds are now draping the once shining sky;
And little I heed how the dreary days go,
Or the dead earth now lying deep under the snow.
We'll heap the bright fire still higher and higher,
And let the wild winds sweep along in their ire!
With the warmth that's within by the red fire's glow,
We heed not the dead earth lying under the snow.
We'll let the sky frown on the Ice-King's cold pomp,
While we sit by the light of our own cheerful lamp.
The flowers sweetly sleep in a drear, darksome grave,
And the hoarse winds above them now mutter and rave;
All the last summer's color, its warmth and its glow,
Are sleeping beneath the pure, beautiful snow.
Yet float down, O snow, from the pure realms of love
To the dead earth beneath from the dim sky above.
With all thy cold blustering, dearly thou art
Enshrined with the image of cheer in each heart;

With the merry sleigh-ride, with the skaters' loud song,
As on steel-bounden feet they glide gaily along.
So we will not repine; by sure tokens we know
That the flowers are but sleeping far down 'neath the snow.
The splendors of springtime are coming again,
And the violet and crocus shall rise from the plain;
And the strong fetters forged by the dread Ice-King's hand,
In his rough, rocky forts in the chilly north-land,
Will be quickly dissolved by the spring's genial breath,
And the grim, discrowned King sleep the still sleep of death.

STANDING ON THE BEACH.

I STAND alone on the beach to-night,
And list to the breakers' roar;
And watch the tall and stately ships,
As they glide away from shore.
And thus I think as I stand alone
And watch the ships receding—
"This,—this is a type of all my hopes
And my desolate heart now bleeding!"

Thus we sail along on life's fair sea,
All outwardly calm and smiling;
Yet God alone knows the inner wreck
Of the hopes that were so beguiling.
So God alone knows how in this sea,
Danger and death are lurking;
Or how soon this gallant craft may be
A thing for the wrecker's working.

The hopes I cherished,—one by one
  In silence I saw them leave me,
There is nothing, or no one under the sun,
  With power henceforth to grieve me.
My heart and hopes alike are crushed,
  But 'tis only an inward bleeding;
And all outside is fair and bright
  As I watch the ships receding.

Now, Father above! Thou God of love!
  Do Thou my vow record!
No idol's worship henceforth is mine,
  I bow to the living Lord!
To none but God do I bend my knee,
  On my heart no flame is feeding;
It flickered and died, my hopes beside,
  As I watched the ships receding.

IN MY GARDEN.

A hum of murmurous insects fills the soft, sweet summer air;
A breath of Heaven floats among the trees,
That, burdened with bright blossoms, bend above with blessings rare,
And flutter forth their fragrance to the breeze.

The soft, green sward below is decked with dandelions gay,
And clover blooms are starting here and there:
For the summer queen is wooing them their beauties to display,
And deepen the ambrosia in the air.

All nature gives her tribute—the swallows skimming
fleet,
The robin chirps upon the blossomed bough;
The humming-bird darts quickly from sweet to fresher
sweet;
Deep in the flowers' heart the bees buzz now.

Ah, who can picture all earth's brightening joys, or dear
delight?
Each hour brings fresh enjoyment to the eyes;
Each day the earth is gladdened with new music, and
each night
Is filled with moonlight smile and dreamy sighs—

Sighs for the morning, when the new world once again
Dawns, deepening all the glorious day before;
And thoughts and feelings holy are filling heart and
brain,
And heaping up life's pleasures more and more.

The lake lies in the distance, a light haze o'er it spread;
Dimly, as through a veil can we descry
The ships that float upon it, their white wings wide
bespread,
To woo the wanton breeze that wanders nigh.

So still, so sweet, so soothing, yet so full of life and love,
This May-day near June's borders seems to be,
That I could lie and listen, and deem myself above
In that wondrous land from care and sorrow free.

Alas, the moments fly! youth and spring are flitting by,
And birds, and bee, and flower will soon be gone;
Then let us enjoy our May, and be happy light and gay,
Fill each day with new delight, ere night comes on.

The present is our own, the past forever flown ;
The future with its burden none may know ;
Let us enjoy our May, life cannot all be gay ;
Let us pluck the sweets and flowers that along our pathway grow.

BUT YESTERDAY.

'TWAS long ago!
No, no!
Love, 'twas but yesterday!
And yet, so far away it seems,
So dimly comes to me in dreams,
That ages might have come and gone
Since last you left me here, alone!

You loved me, then!
Ah, when?
Love, 'twas but yesterday!
Loved? now you love no more!
Hark! hear the lake's loud roar!
'Tis the surf, madly beating
The rocks and then retreating.
Do the rocks yield? Ah, never!
Rocks are but rocks, forever!

Dost seek to wound?
No sound!
Love, 'twas but yesterday!
But love has wings and flies,
And the heart wounded dies;
And though I beat, and beat against the rocks,
My heart alone can feel the cruel shocks!

The dream was sweet,
Though fleet.
Love, 'twas but yesterday
You held me in strong, loving arms,
And, smiling, kissed away alarms,
And soothed my fears, and dried my tears;
Oh, the joy of the long vanished years!

Can I forget?
Not yet!
Love, 'twas but yesterday.
So sweet the dreams yet hold,
More precious than fine gold.
You wooed me and you won me! vain regret—
Had you not won me, you had wooed me yet!

IN THE BLOSSOMED CHESTNUT.

In the blossomed chestnut where the bees sing,
Humming birds flutter, and every happy thing
Dances in the sunshine sifted through the leaves,
Looking down with laughing eyes where a fairy weaves
Dainty threads of gossamer over all the grass,
Just to catch the dew-drops as night shadows pass—
Robin redbreast, golden oriole, darting with quick wing,
In the blossomed chestnut where the bees sing!

Lilies bursting into bloom just across the way;
Mountain ash and maple pennons wide display;
Flowers scattered everywhere, filling all the air
With a fresher fragrance, and a beauty rare;

Nature's robe of emerald, worn with queenly grace,
For the sunny smiling June that beautifies her face;
Every wanton wind that blows deeper raptures bring
To the bonny chestnuts where the bees sing!

Surely such a sight as this makes sadness flee away;
Who could mope and mutter 'gainst fate on such a day,
When the very fact of living is in itself a bliss,
When the earth and sky commingle, and lake and cloud-
let kiss;
When entrancing strains of music and contentment fill
the air,
From all the skyey dwellers, and love seems everywhere;
And we lift our hearts to Heaven in thanks for simple
things,
Like bird and bee and blossom that the bonny chestnut
brings!

LONGING.

WHERE the summer sun is glowing,
And the gentle breeze is blowing,
And the tall trees shadows throwing
On the grassy lea,
Here I sit and ponder,
While I long to wander
By the silver sea.

Here the dusky pine uplifteth
Boughs through which the sunlight sifteth;
And the wind its dead leaves drifteth
O'er the lonely land;
There the palm tree's top is waving,
And the silver sea is laving
All the golden sand.

Oh, I hear its voice of gladness,
Drowning every note of sadness,
And all melancholy madness,
In its lowly hum;
Saying when the waves are rushing
Fierce, or with calm music gushing,
"Worn and wearied, come!"

JUST AT THE END OF THE ROAD.

JUST at the end of the road the lake lies silent and dim,
Behind a mysterious misty veil that shrouds the distant rim
Where sky and water meet, and far beyond our ken,
Seem to mingle in peace, never to part again.

Just at the end of the road passes a slow-moving train.
No sound of the wheel on the rail. I bend and hearken in vain.
No whistle for "down brakes" now, no hiss of escaping steam
Is heard. From where my vision strikes, no fire-eyed engines gleam.

Just at the end of the road—and green fields lie between—
Telegraph poles show sharp defined against a dull, dead sky.
All beyond is misty and dull as in a dream,
As if behind that wall of white a far-off fate may lie!

Just at the end of the road! Ah me, a funeral passed to-day—
Solemn, slow-moving and silent, the cortege wended its way.

Eighty-eight years had the old man carried his weary
load,
Laying his burden down gladly, just at the end of the
road!

Just at the end of the road! O, what lies there for me?
Travail and toil and trouble along the way I see;
But the sting of scorn, the stint of fame, anxious
Ambition's goad,
Gone will be and forgotten, just at the end of the road.

Birds sing, buds bloom, the apple boughs fling fragrant
petals far,
And beauty bends benignly from bright moon and flashing star;
But I, alone and lonely, long for that blest abode
In the land beyond the misty veil, just at the end of the
road!

A SUMMER MEMORY.

How beautiful it was, that calm night in July,
When the moon, round and white, was sailing high
Upon a heaven as pure as God's own face;
Of cloud or trouble there was not a trace.

There was no eye to mark, no ear to hear
The love you looked, the words you whispered, dear;
All earth was ours, ours was the heaven, too,
In which the moon hung, bright and fair to view.

The tall, old trees that lined the village street,
Made fitful shades round our soft-falling feet;
The whispering leaves for once forgot their tale,
And left no murmurs on the evening gale.

The people were in bed ; good sooth to say,
Had they been up, it had not been that way ;
People were made to talk, and birds to fly,
And love for moonlight walks in warm July !

And so the romance faded ! yet the bliss
Lies in our hearts from that long, loving kiss !
All else forgotten—world and stars and moon,
Save the thought-torturing—we part so soon !

'Tis winter now, again the moon sails high,
Yet coldly shines, as dead love's distant eye.
We're parted ! Hard for hearts with love once smitten,
But the bard sings : "Love's vows in snow are written !"

A JUNE MORNING.

The dews that gem the eyes of morn
Lie lovingly upon the rose ;
A scent of summer, rich and warm,
Through all the air divinely blows.

The locust, lifting creamy blooms,
The snowdrops, rearing round white heads,
Give forth their glorious perfumes
To rouse the dreamers from their beds.

The morning air is sweet with sound,
With song of bird and hum of bee ;
With rush of swallow soaring high,
Then wheeling low upon the lea.

The rosy clouds of morn lie curled,—
Like childhood's sunny locks they lie
Over the brow of the blind half-world,
Waiting the promise from on high.

Slowly the Monarch comes in sight;
The birds burst forth in fresher song,
Carolling loudly to the light
Which lark and robin waited long.

The rose shakes off her tear-gemmed veil;
The bee takes wandering wing afar;
The violet blue and daisy pale
Open their petals to the air.

Each bird and bee, each bud and flower,
Unite in sweetest song, to raise
At this pure, winsome, wildering hour,
A pean to their Maker's praise.

HODIE MIHI.

I SAID, "To-day is mine!" I will enjoy
The loving, lingering moments ere they leave;
The hopes, the friendships that will not deceive.
Though other lights may lure, and loves decoy,
My soul stands sure on this her steadfast rock,
Safely withstanding storms and tempests' shock;
Though clouds may darken, or suns burning shine,
To-day is mine!

And so, I steered my ship o'er smiling seas,
And love lay cradled in the laughing breeze
That rocked the restless bosom of the deep ;
And all the mermaidens that lie asleep
Upon their coral couches all the day,
Roused their restless charms to wile away
The love I deemed my own in storm or shine,—
That love of mine !

Ah, who can claim an hour as their own ?
A moment's merry play of careless laughter,
And tears and travail follow fast thereafter ;
And joy is broken by a grievous groan ;
And love, at sight of tears or sound of sighing,
Uses the wings were given him for flying,
Waiting for fairer skies and suns to shine,
This day of mine !

Let no man plume himself upon the past,
Or count caresses which to-morrow brings ;
The bird which on the wood-top trills and sings
Flies from the northern tempest far and fast,
And seeks a sunnier, smiling, southern clime,
And sweetly sings, forgetful of the time
When love and youth and blissful "Auld lang syne."
Were thine and mine !

Beloved, in the days when life was young
We counted not the cost of anything ;
Our fancies mounted high as lark on wing,
And, like the lark, our blithe glad voices rung ;
And, with youth's confidence in coming pleasure,
We sang unstinted, joyous beyond measure ;
Care could not cloud us, nor grief make us pine,
That day of mine !

Ah, well! 'Tis only that we feel too keen
The loss of friendship that we never owned;
The calumny and censure now condoned;
Have been allowed to "peep behind the scene,"
And see how friendship's flimsy robe was made,
And the deceitful hearts of those who played,—
To see thy pleasures pall and love decline,
O, day of mine!

Why must we sigh and sob o'er dead love's bier?
Leaves fall, and trees stand shrunken, brown and bare;
But there is promise in the frosty air
That sap shall stir, and leaf and bud appear,
And clothe the naked limbs with life once more:
But love, once dead, no power can restore;
'Tis only memory gives us gall for wine.—
Dead love of mine!

DO YOU REMEMBER?

Clouds are the etchings of God's hand
Upon the sky's bright scroll;
No human hand can draw those lines,
And such bright forms unroll.

* * * *

Clouds, like banners half unrolled,
Tipped with crimson, purple, gold,
Flung athwart a cool gray sky,
Meet the poet's raptured eye.

Fades the sunset, fades the glow!
Clouds of sorrow, clouds of woe,
Dun and dim, foreboding strife,
Flung athwart the poet's life!

Friend of mine! in after days
When clouds like these meet thy gaze,
Memory shall gleam and shine
With a radiance half divine.

Gleams of glory! Puffs of air!
Glow and fade, no longer there.
Only memory can trace
When last year's joys had place!

IN MEMORIAM.

Col. A. T. H. Williams, M.P.,

Died at Batoche, buried July 21st, 1885, at Port Hope, on the day his troops were welcomed home publicly.

Low lies the hero, and tears fall like rain,
Never he'll come to his loved ones again.
Stricken in battle? Nay, harder the blow!
After the victory thus he's laid low.
Loyal hearts, one and all, look we to you,
Give him a welcome, "Tender and True!"

Streamlets that murmur and sing in your glee,
On your glad way to the broad-bosomed sea,
Carry with you on your devious way
The wail from the hearts of the people to-day.
Nothing can equal the grief now his due;
Weep for him, mourn for him, "Tender and True."

Beautiful song birds, sing 'round his grave,
Gently, ye branches, over him wave ;
Bees in the clover that cover the sod,
Droning sweet music, " Gone to his God."
All things beneath the skies bright and blue,
Give him a welcome, " Tender and True."

Sing him sweet lullabies in his low bed,
Evening dews, down-dropping, cover his head ;
Blow, softest breezes, summer's sweet breath,
Never lay man so lamented in death !
Noble life found him, life is passed through,
Angels now welcome him, " Tender and True ! "

WILLIAMS.

Written for the unveiling of his monument at Port Hope, on September 4th, 1889.

THOU hast thy glories, gory-headed war !
The charging squadrons, and the scream and hiss
Of many hurtling shot, but only Peace
    Can bring a day like this.

A moving mass of men and women thronged
To hear the words which consecrate for aye,
A martyr's monument in our memories,
    On this memorial day :

A proud memento, which the faithful love
And admiration which his country gives
To all her honoured dead. Long as this stands,
    Williams, thy memory lives !

Where Canada's defenders, winged with scars,
Soar through the azure fields of endless stars,
Thy soul still lives, and, bending down to earth,
Marks all our solemn mirth.

Death he sought often on the battle-field,
When British valor made the dark foe yield,
But not in battle did his mighty soul
Go down to death—ah, heavy dole!

Yet none the less a hero brave he stands,
This statue, reared by loving comrades' hands,
Tells that he met death bravely when it came,
With his great heart aflame!

Face to face, fighting as for country's need,
So shall our children as its lines they read,
Learn how the hero-martyr met his fate—
Williams, thy meed of praise is great!

THE RIVER OF LIFE.

A WIDE, dark stream, whose swollen flood
Draws downward to a precipice;
And ships, with sails and streamers set,
Rush headlong towards the dread abyss.
On either side the river, rise
Tall mountains, towering to the skies.

The storm-rocked stream roars rough and rude,
And throws up seething, hissing spray;
But on its breast ride vessels good,

Holding the thoughtless and the gay—
Ships laden with a motley throng,
O'er the surgy stream they dash along.

Fame—brilliant vessel—dashes by!
How dazzling every face appears!
A smiling face, a flashing eye,
But a heart choked with sorrow's tears!
Ah, sons of Song! Ah, ship of Fame!
How much ye dare for a deathless name!

Wealth, holding heavy heaps of care,
Sails statelily upon the stream;
And gems and diamonds, rich and rare,
Flash o'er the wave with brilliant beam.
Ah, souls, who on this vessel wait,
Your cargo gains not Heaven's gate!

Pleasure—a pretty, jaunty craft,
Holding a merry, witty throng;
Hear ye not the light, careless laugh,
The sparkling jest, the joyful song
Gay moths, who flutter in the beam,
Nor know the end of this dark stream.

Are all as thoughtless of the end?
Are all as careless of the storm?
No! on the deck of each strong ship
Kneels many a weary, fainting form.
" Father," they pray, " avert the fate,
The agonies that for us wait."

Behold upon the banks above,
A blessed, matchless form appears;
He throws the cords of faith and love,

They grasp, and soon are dried their tears.
"Praise God," they sing; "join comrades all,
Make safety sure, and on Him call."

Have faith and fear not. Say to Him:
"Remove from me my cause of grief!
Father, in Thee I full believe;
Help, Christ, help Thou mine unbelief!"
No more than this does He require—
No less can man, if sane, desire.

O, soul! storm-stricken on Life's stream,
Lift up thine eyes to Him who stands
Upon the banks where sunlight gleams,
And time rolls on with golden sands.
No storm, no sorrow, sickness, strife,
But glorious and eternal life!

THE DYING DAY.

THE day is dying in the west and darkest night comes on,
The night "when no man worketh," and life and hope are gone;
Gone to the past whose gleaming gates are closed on them for aye,
And we sob and sigh till night wears off and dawns another day.

I saw it when the sleepy clouds of morn lay lightly curled
In crimson waves above the brow of the half-blind wintry world;

I watched it dawn and deepen on to full and perfect day,
And night's dark clouds and shadows fled before the
sun's bright ray.

And thus, I thought, though dark despair and clouds of
deepest night,
Hover above our earthly path and keep us from the
light,
Yet some day will the sun of hope and happiness arise,
And drive the darkness from our hearts, the shadows
from our eyes.

It may, it must, be that life's woes are sent to us in love,
To loose the heart from earthly things and fix the faith
above.
Yet, Father, give us love below, nor make our path so
drear,
That we should long for death because life holds for us
no cheer.

I cannot kiss the rod that smites; I want the loving
hand
Laid kindly on my burning brow, and not a stern com-
mand.
Ah! tell me not that God is pleased not to be loved but
feared;
That not by us to be adored, only to be revered.

The creeds of men will tell us to hold our God in awe;
To reverence His holy word, and keep His written law;
The creed of Christ says unto all: "See ye love one
another,
But love God most of all, and love Me as an Elder
Brother."

OUR GOOD QUEEN.

May 24th, 1885.

Once more this day returns to us,
  Clothed with earth's choicest green;
And flowers fair, both rich and rare,
  On every side are seen.
And perfume-laden breezes sigh,
  Ecstatic as they play,
Seeking with blessings bright to crown
  Our good Queen's natal day!

Then shout for Queen Victoria,
  Long may she live and reign,
And many years bring back to her
  Her natal day again.

Her reign with blessings has been fraught,
  And subjects free and glad
Praise her laws good and merciful—
  Such laws ne'er Britain had!
But, more than this! we honor her,
  We hold her dear as life,
The queen and crown of womanhood,
  Pure mother, perfect wife!

Then shout for Queen Victoria,
  Long may she live and reign,
May many years bring back to her
  Her natal day again!

Then shout aloud for our good Queen,
  And all our hearts be gay,
As here we meet to celebrate
  Our Sovereign's natal day.

Thank God for Queen Victoria!
The best the world has seen,
And may each heart put forth its prayer—
God guard our gracious Queen!

Then shout for Queen Victoria!
Long may she live and reign,
And many years bring back to her
Her natal day again!

NELSON.

I STOOD within the solemn cloistered stillness
Of an old church, gray with the dust of years,
And marked the many monuments of men,
By which their country, for whose common weal
They lived, and loved, and died, them glorified
In gleaming marble or in burnished brass.
A group of four fixed wondering my gaze;
Foremost of these was Nelson, whose proud name,
For daring and devotion to his duty,
Has long years reigned a revered household word
In stately English homes, and, too, in those
Of other climes and names. Beside him stood
A gleaming figure, as an angel clad
In flowing vestures, and with finger raised
And pointed to the statue at her side;
Admonishing two peasant lads who stand
And gaze admiringly upon the hero,
To emulate his virtues, and his brave
And gallant life, and meet, as chance they may,
His glorious death, and fair, proud, spotless fame,
Unending yet. So shall the sons of England's soil

Be to their country's Queen, and quiet homes
As bulwarks beaten by an angry wind ;
Or like the chalk cliffs of their lovely isle,
Though buffeted by waves and rudest winds,
Stand statelily and firm, and fear no foe.
And so, methought, the Christian, in his course,
Though buffeted by cruel winds of scorn,
And maligned motives, and drawbacks of ill,
Is pointed by his guardian angel's hand
(Who, standing, watches all his hopes and fears,
His fair temptations and his foulest sins),
To Christ, the Master, in His high abode,
Who once was man below and felt the woe
And trials of the flesh, yet sinnèd not,
Whispers with silver softness in his ear:
" Be like Him ! strive to reach that eminence
Whereon He sits enthroned, a God indeed,
By doing as He did, and putting on,
Like as it were a garment, the whole life
And glowing virtues and the saving grace
Of man's best model, Christ, the living God !"

FOR MY PASTOR.

Written on the occasion of a celebration of a ten years' pastora of Rev. A. A. Drummond, C.P. Church, Newcastle.

How little reck we of the time that glides
Away so swiftly, yet with stealthy feet !
We tread the paths that yesterday we trod,
But yesterday we never more can meet.
If time were told by heart-beats, what long years
For some are pent within the decade past !
But sunniest joy, or sorrow's deepest wave,
Love's raptures, or dire hate, will rarely last ten years !

Within that space, how many faces known,
And forms, how loved, have low been laid to rest!
'Twas hard to miss the dear ones; yet we know
Who rules all things still judges for us best.
On some the years have lightly lain, and seem
Like glittering gems from Time's fair finger flung.
The while they walked in blossomed woodland bowers,
And heard sweet songs by lute-toned warblers sung.

Fair white-winged ships filled with rich argosies,
From each heart's port put out to seas all calm;
Fair winds may waft them on their homeward course,
Breathing of spicy groves and pine and palm;
But storms may rise upon the smoothest seas,
And barks are wrecked and strewn upon the strand,
And white, wild faces watch their ships engulfed,
And fond hopes shattered, within sight of land!

How happy he to whom the boon is given
To know his labours never end in naught!
To find a ladder that leads up to Heaven
Formed, round on round, of good deeds fairly wrought.
To feel each hour a pearl on silken string
By loving fingers placed, and pure with joy,
Shining like plumes upon an angel's wing,
Pleasures that never pall, nor dross alloy!

Such bliss, my pastor, may be yours to-day!
A life well lived, some decades of good deeds,
A broad humanity that ne'er forgets
That flowers may oft be found among the weeds!
That stoops from high estate and priestly garb,
To lift the lowly to a higher plane,
Strengthen the weak, and check the erring soul,
Despising social place and worldly gain!

Long may the earthly church that owns you head,
Feel the sweet sway that over them is set;
And the next decade bring you added joys
Of work well done, of crown well won; and yet
A higher joy may sheep and shepherd share,
When, after toil and trouble, joy and pain,
We reach the "Church triumphant" "over there,"
Pastor and people may unite again!

LEAVE ME NOT YET.

LEAVE me not yet! The hours go by in sadness,
The night is dark, no light comes with the morn;
With thee will flee all love and hope and gladness,
Leaving me wretched, lonely and forlorn!

Leave me not yet! I waste my heart in sighing,
Clinging unto thy lips in perfect bliss;
Gazing into thine eyes, I would be dying,
If death could bring me such a joy as this!

Leave me not yet! Clasp thy fond arms about me,
And let me breathe in Heaven a little while;
Bend the full gaze of thy blue eyes upon me,
And sun me in thine ever-loving smile!

How can I let thee go? Stay yet a minute
To whisper words we never can forget!
Each moment hath an age of rapture in it,—
I cannot let thee go! Leave me not yet!

IN A LILY'S CUP.

A LONG, green stem creeps out from the brown earth,
And broad leaves, coarsely veined, come with its birth.
But at its topmost end, a sheath of white
Unfolding, shows a bud of beauty bright.
Fair, pure, and stainless, fed by warmth and glow
Within, though all without is draped in snow;
A hot-house flower, preserved from storm or cold,
It lives, grows, blossoms, and then waxes old.
Its life is brief, but beautiful. Look deep
Within its calyx as it lies asleep,
I'll read you there in rhyme, this dreary day,
But whether "song or sermon" you shall say.

Hear how the mad, weird March winds rave and roar.
See the surf, beating on the rock-crowned shore;
You cannot feel the cruel, biting blast,
It shakes your windows, as it hurries past;
But you are housed and fed, and safe within
A lily's cup, stainless and free from sin.

Its white walls of pure influence close you round;
Within its sheltered heart you love have found;
And "passion's host, that never brooked control,"
Ne'er storms the citadel of saintly soul.
You have felt pain, and who that lives has not?
Such pain as nature renders common lot;
But sorrow for lost hope, lost love, or sin,
Has ne'er your lily's portals entered in;
Sorrow for others, for a world sin-cursed,
Such of all sorrow seems to you the worst.

Look from your window, where the lilies bloom,
And fragrance of sweet flowers scents the room,—
And rags and wretchedness may smite the eye
That lights alone for beauty, you may sigh,—
For purest pity pearls the lily's heart,
And prompts the tears that from its eyelids start.
But ne'er those eyes can weep such tears as flow
From those who know the depths of want and woe,
And ne'er the heart can comprehend the sin,
That to the lily never entered in.
The world is sinful, you may say, and yet
O'er far off heathen you may sigh and fret,
But do not know, or do not understand
There are worse than heathen in the land.
"Unto the pure all things are pure," and so
The lily's cup is pure as unsunned snow.
Its heart's sweet innocence, its home of love,
Its likeness here below to Heaven above.
Safe from rude winds, its sweetness folded up,
Best of all dwellings is a lily's cup!

THE SHOWER.

MAJESTIC masses, clouds of dun, columned and still, they stood,
Then rolled along the horizon and rested o'er the wood;
And from their dark capacious depths came forth a heavy shower,
Deluging every bud and branch and every leaf and flower.

The robin sheltered in her nest but little recked the storm;
Her little broodlings 'neath her breast were cuddled safe and warm;

Her mate upon a tall pine tree sat 'neath a branch low hung,
And from his perch called cheerfully to mother and her young.

A little time, and then afar pranced all the steeds of air;
The mighty monarch of the day shone peacefully and fair
Upon a scene but lately strewn with wrecks of branch and flower,
Which the bold storm-king dashed aside, the playthings of an hour.

A little time again, and then the flowers raised their heads,
And rested gracefully reclined upon their mossy beds;
The robin made the wild woods ring with soul-entrancing song,
And all the stagnant streams of life rolled peacefully along.

AT HOREB'S ROCK.

SEE the thirsty souls draw nigh!
Hark the deep despairing cry:
"Give us water, Moses, water!
Give us water or we die!"
Ah, the sight was desolate.
For the famished people wait,
For the rain that never cometh,
For the stream that never runneth,
For some little trickling rill,
At the foot of some great hill.
Where their fever-palsied lips
Once more at the fountain sip.

Strong men groaned in anguish wild,
Mothers held a feeble child,
Whose parched lips and glassy eye
Spoke the fell Destroyer nigh.
"Courage!" Moses said, "we soon
Shall have water, and ere noon
Reach we Horeb's rock and see
Water gushing full and free!
Priests and Elders, follow me,
Thus the Lord commandeth thee!"
Read we the old story still,
How that Moses smote the rock,
How it yielded to the shock,
Cleft its side, and gushing free,
Water spouted! Water! See,
See the thirsty myriads drink,
See them throng about the rill
Trickling down upon the sward—
Women panted, "Praise the Lord!"

See the Saviour on the tree!
See Him writhe in agony!
See His piercèd hands and side!
Christ, the Rock, is crucified!
See the blood and water flow
Down on sinners bending low,
That a weary world, sin-curst,
May o'ercome their maddening thirst;
May here drink and ever be
Free from sin and misery.
Come and drink ye wavering ones!
Come, ye whom the Saviour owns!
Come, ye weary, sin-opprest,
Let your burdened souls find rest!

See the stream that issues free,
Drink and no more thirsty be!
Hearts harder far than Horeb's rock,
Rent asunder by the shock,
By the lightning of Thy Word,—
Save them, draw them, Christ our Lord.

INVOCATION.

Sleep softly, sunbeams, on his grave
Under the prairie grass;
Tall, flaunting flowers over him wave,
And droop as the hours pass.

Lie warm and bright on his narrow bed,
Weave him an amber shroud;
All gorgeous colors over him shed
From the prairie sunset's cloud.

Sing lowly, zephyrs, your anthems grand,
Like the song at evening sung
By his cradle, rocked by a mother's hand,
When life for him was young.

Moonbeams, your softest lustre shed,
Your silver shimmering fling
Over my darling's low, lone bed,
Like the plumes from an angel's wing.

All things beautiful, bright and good,
Compass him all around;
While I weep in my woeful widowhood,
With my pale face pressed to the ground.

I LAY ME DOWN TO SLEEP.

I LAY me down to sleep!
With airs from Eden-land
My burning brow is fanned;
And summer silence deep,
Waveth o'er all its wand.

I lay me down to sleep!
And yet it is not night,
For all around is bright;
But o'er my eyes doth creep
That which denies them sight.

I lay me down to sleep!
Pray God I wake again
Where I shall feel no pain;
And death's cool slumber deep
Fall soft as summer rain.

MY OLD HOME.

I LONG for a look at my dear old home,
Which the spring-time has scented so sweet;
I long for a view of Ontario's blue
That stretches away at its feet.
Its hillsides all covered with clover,
Where the honey-bees live in a dream;
Its valleys that lie to the blue sunny sky,
While wild-flowers line the banks of the stream.

The oak and the maple stand proudly,
  And guard its green meadows and slopes;
The beech and the poplar give shelter
  To the robin who trills out his hopes.
The ivy and bittersweet cling to the boughs
  Of the basswoods that grow by the brook;
The touch-me-nots cluster in silver and green,
  In the depths where the sun dares not look.

How oft have I sat in my own little nook,
  Where the soft green sward gave back no sound,
And bathed my tired soul in the freshness of earth,
  While the fragrance of flowers floated round.
No one spot to me can e'er so dear be
  As that nook in the bosom of the hills,
Shut out from man's ken and the sun's glaring eye,
  By humility—safe from all ills.

MY SOUTHLAND.

My soul is away in the Southland to-day!
  There, lying 'mid heavenly calm,
I am watching the white-clouds that overhead stray,
  And breathing the zephyrs of balm;
And while my eyes scan the wild landscape without,
  There nought of discomfort I find,
Though the storm-demon rides with a laugh and a shout,
  Borne about in the arms of the wind.

The snow piled on high, the dull leaden sky,
  No chill to my soul-dream can give;
While the fire glows bright on my heart and my hearth,
  'Tis joy but to love and to live.

And I heed not the storm or the chill winter blast,
For the future this promise bestows;
My Southland will come when the winter is past,
And the summer will bring back the rose.

Not the rose that is gone. That can never again
To the light of the summer return;
But the fire of that love that glows bright in our hearts
Can nevermore cease there to burn:
For love is eternal! So linger we here
In the northland of ice and of snow,
Nor sigh for the Southland while love gives the cheer,
That the heart makes its own roses blow!

WHAT SHALL I OFFER THEE?

WHAT shall I offer thee? Gems and gold?
Wealth in abundance, treasures untold?
Or the wealth of a love that shall never grow cold?

What shall I tell thee? That riches and power,
And beauty have rendered thee their fairest dower?
Or that day by day I shall love thee more?

What shall I say to convince thee I love thee?
Say that thou'rt fair as the bright sky above thee
Studded with stars? Or say simply: I love thee?

O, not by loud vows is sweet love to be won,
Nor wooings from morning to setting of sun,
I say to thee, sweetest, I love thee alone!

O, BONNY MOON!

O, I WAIT and watch and listen,
While the stars so brightly glisten,
For a footstep that I know is coming soon;
Bend thee down in all thy glory,
From thy height to list the story
That hath been so often told beneath thy light,
O, bonny moon!

O, my heart is wildly beating,
At the rapture of the meeting,
And the waves are murmuring a softened croon;
Now they beat the beach in gladness,
Now retreating moan in sadness,
So ebbs and flows my heart's red tide to-night,
O, bonny moon!

Each sweet bird hath sought its nest,
All the world is hushed to rest,
Save whip-poor-will that singeth his sad tune;
Lone he sings and lone I wait,
For I fear me he is late,
And I want thy rays to light him to my arms,
O, bonny moon!

So I sang one summer even,
Till the moon rode high in Heaven,
And my heart drank in the loveliness of moonlight, youth and June;
But the beautiful June morrow
Brought me much of woe and sorrow,
Sorrow for my love that met me 'neath thy light,
O, bonny moon!

Was it but a premonition,
Or some angel intuition,
That taught me to be sad yet glad in singing my love tune?
He who sat with me that even,
The next morning was in heaven,
And no sadder heart than mine now beats beneath
The bonny moon!

So I linger, old and weary,
And the time drags slow and dreary,
But there will come a time, my love,—
And Heaven send it soon!
When beside thee I shall slumber,
And with thee be of the number
Who delight in blessing loving hearts who meet
Beneath the moon!

DEATH.

"Out of the shadows of sadness."

Ah, could we but be certain,
That when we lift the curtain
About us, and fall asleep,
We should go from sorrow and tears,
To a land full of hope, free from fears;
Nevermore to awake and weep.

Would our ship always calmly sail,
Untouched by tempestuous gale,
Over silent and sapphire seas?
Would the spices of summer e'er breathe
Around us, above us, beneath;
Unchilled by the cold winter breeze?

Do the flowers wear bright faces alway?
Is it always and ever glad-day?
  Does there never come night nor rain?
Do the leaves never fall from the trees?
Does there never on anyone seize
  Sadness nor sickness nor pain?

Does never descend the snow?
Do never the cold winds blow?
  Is it always warm and light?
Take me there, then, O, Death!
Pityingly pluck away breath,
  Take me where there is no night!

I am so weary of life,
Weary of sorrow and strife,
  Glad when the day is done;
The day of this world gone by,
The record written on high,
  And I so much nearer the throne!

Nearer the pitying Friend,
Who some day will graciously end
  This medley of all things sad;
This picture that pleaseth awhile,
This scene of a tear and a smile,
  This song that is good and bad.

And I, so sorrowful, say:
I am sick of the world's sad day,
  I am sick of the weary night;
I am tired of sorrow and pain,
I am weary of sunshine and rain,
  I am weary of darkness and light!

JESSIE.

ANGELS in heaven, sound your harps of gold!
  Wave your bright wings, and fan the perfumed air
To sweeter fragrance! Here our world is cold—
  The flowers are gone, and trees are getting bare!

Ye choir of cherubims! your sweetest songs
  Sing loud, in honor of an angel's birth!
Down here, where all things right are seeming wrongs,
  We call it death, with moan in place of mirth!

But there, up there, where heart speaks out to heart,
  And all is warmth and light and love and praise;
Where no wrong comes, no sickness, no more pain,
  Nor heartache, sorrow, night—but all bright days.

Why should we mourn when angel bands rejoice
  To welcome home another angel-child?
Why grieve to know another angel voice
  Has joined the cherub choir all undefiled?

How hath He honored them, to whom was given
  The care of a bright jewel for His crown!
How hath He trusted, when, though ripe for heaven,
  He left them golden sheaves so long unbound?

The "Happy Land," to her once far away,
  To which she called to all her friends to "come,"
She sings with sweeter voice in heaven to-day
  Than she could do in this her earthly home!

The little pain-tossed casket is at rest,
  That held the sweet spirit for such weary days;
The little hands are folded on her breast,
  The beauteous curls still cluster round her face.

Angels, with welcome meet her at the gates!
  Seraphs, your sweetest airs about her play!
For many years she has been fit for heaven,
  But darling Jessie's just gone home to-day!

FOR KITTY.

O, BLUE eyes closed for evermore!
  O, folded hands, that lie so still,
Like chiselled marble, on the breast
  That feels nor joy nor ill.

O, hair of gold, that kissed a brow
  Fairer than aught can be of earth;
So fair, we know that angels sealed
  Thee for their own at birth!

O, lips that nevermore may speak
  The loving words we long to hear,
Or ringing laughter, that proclaimed
  Our merry Kitty near!

O, little feet, that ever ran
  To meet us at the open door;
The joyous shout, the clinging hand,
  Will greet us nevermore!

O, never more shall we behold
  The form we thought so full of grace,
Or see the light we loved so well
  Upon that sweet young face!

To us 'tis always young! The years
  That roll may earthly features change;
But she will ever be as now—
  Her steps no further range!

MEMENTO MORI.

HEAVILY fell the snow
Over the dead earth below,
Drifted and piled in heaps of purest white;
The wild wind shrieked and wailed,
And a cheek with death was paled,
For a life was ebbing fast away that night.

Heavily fell the snow,
Piling in heaps below,
Over the ruined gables brown and bare;
Quietly ebbed the breath
Of the form stricken in death.
Whose breath was cold as coldest winter air.

Quietly fell the morn,
Calmly slept the storm,
And the God of day smiled sweetly on the scene;
Sweetly as if no woe
Had fallen with the snow
Upon the house where sickness long had been.

Gently her form was laid
Into its snowy bed,
Cold as the mantle which wrapped the cold earth ;
Snow cold in snow,
Lowered below,
Never to rise till the glorious new birth.

Mother, we miss thee!
Yearn to caress thee!
Sweet be thy sleep in the cold, snowy grave;
There will we leave thee
Till God receive thee,
While round thy pillow the winter winds rave.

THE HIDDEN GRAVE

THERE'S a grave, lone and dark, dug deep out of sight,
Where no grass ever grows,
Where no blossom e'er blows;
All is barren and cold, though bright-winged birds sing;
And blade, bud and bloom from the forest glades spring.

A weak woman's hands dug that grave, lone and dark!
In the still hours of night,
'Neath the moon's ghostly light,
She visits that grave, and, alone, lifts the lid
And looks on the lost one her own hands have hid.

A tall, manly form in that coffin is laid;
A broad brow, deathly fair,
From which pale golden hair
Is combed back, but the lids o'er the blue eyes are closed,
And the strong, shapely hands on the breast are reposed.

No eye, save the All-Seeing One, looks upon
This lone grave that is kept
By a woman's hand, wept
By a woman's tears only, and they fall unseen ;
While a laugh or a jest fill the spaces between.

You wonder, perhaps, where this lone grave is made ;
Who coffined the dead
There so peacefully laid ;—
Many bright eyes may seem in gay scenes to take part,
Many gay smiles may cover a grave in the heart.

WAITING.

The cold winds of winter are wailing
Above Minnesota's broad plain,
And the snow-white earth, like a maiden,
Is waiting her lover again.
Like a maiden who waits for her lover,
She waits the embrace of the spring ;
All hushed, though wild winds sweep above her,
She waits for the coming of spring.

They sigh soft as the season advances,
And brings on the balmy-breathed hours ;
And the grass buds, like emerald lances,
Pierce her bosom ; then follow the flowers.
The soft summer hours bring her gladness,
For the rose-encrowned earth reigns a queen,
And the birds and the wild bees pronounce her
The loveliest that ever was seen.

She revels in fulness of pleasure,
  No doubt in her bosom remains;
But, alas for the maiden! her treasure
  Sleeps beneath Minnesota's broad plains.
The breezes of winter or summer
  Unheeded sigh over his head;
Alike are the storm and the sunshine,
  So quietly resteth the dead!

MAYSIE.

Sad, we say, and sigh, as the slow-moving funeral train
Climbs up the bare, brown road, and back to the house on the hill
Is borne the senseless clay, from which through throes of pain,
The suffering saintly soul escaped all earthly ill.

Sad, we say, and sigh. Then back to our day's drear toil,
The struggle for daily bread, the wrestle with daily pain,
Pitying the pure, sweet spirit so free from taint or soil.
Pitying weary pain-racked limbs for finding rest again.

Death is not sad! Rather life—life with its manifold snares—
Life with its perilous pathways, its long, bleak stretches of pain,
Its mountains of wrong, its gulfs of woe, its rocks of dire despair,
Its memories of lost Paradise, its murderer's brand of Cain!

*   *   *   *   *   *   *

Hush! do we dream of life? We have walked awake
with woe.
But the mother-love is hungry, the mother-heart is weak;
Who can comfort the mourner, who dry the tears that
flow,
While we cannot hear for heart-throbs the words our
friends may speak!

Peace! Looks she not lovely? The little lips red as life,
The pure, sweet face, as slumber hath sealed the dark,
brown eyes,
Closed upon earthly woe, and years of ghastly pain,—
Opened to see the forms of those here loved in Paradise.

No, not sad, but joyful! Upborne on glistening wing,
Never to fail nor falter, never to gasp or groan;
There, 'mid the flowers of Eden, only to soar and sing,
Only to lure with beckoning hand the loved ones left
so lone.

Steadily upward, onward! Life is too poor and small
To satisfy the souls of those whose treasures are above,
Or still the infinite longing that lives in the hearts of all
For the bright and beautiful Beyond, where love shall
meet with love.

* * * * * * *

But the last sad rite is over. The solemn words are
said—
"Ashes to ashes" (they falter). "Dust to dust" ('tis
done).
And all that is left of Maysie is laid in the narrow bed.
Peace! It is well! Pray softly for those who are left
alone.

NEWTON HILL.

THERE lieth a city within my sight—
A city whose towers gleam marble white,
A city whose mansions give forth no light,
  Whose streets are deserted and lone;
And the dwellers therein so quietly rest,
With head pillowed softly on Mother Earth's breast;
  And in sleep they make no moan.

A quiet city is that which lies
Within full sight of my aching eyes,
As I watch the day fade from the skies,
  While the twilight lovingly lingers;
The long twilight of a day of rain
Whose pearly drops pelt the window pane
  Like the tapping of skeleton fingers.

Up from the hamlet under the hill
Cometh the sound of hammer and mill;
Men who can work and think with a will,
  The hammer and pen there wield;
Careless of sorrow or wind or rain,
Toiling for naught but the love of gain,
  Unwilling life to yield.

Darkness falls on the emerald earth;
From lighted halls comes the sound of mirth;
Of wine and wassail there is no dearth,
  But the sound of the hammer is still.
Those who wielded it, those who sing,
The pathway of Time will unfailingly bring
  To the city upon the hill.

Erewhile the moonlight in splendor falls
Upon its towers and marble walls,
And one lone bird through the long night calls
  In pitiful song for its mate.
And the silvery faces of moonlit waves,
Singing a requiem o'er deep-dug graves,
  Low down in the valley wait.

OLD LETTERS.

YES, I am burying my dead;
  Burying the lost treasures of my heart!
Pitying the clay-cold forms from which hath fled
  The knowledge of all art.

Yes, there they lie so still,
  With cold hands folded o'er a lifeless breast,
I bend above with face as white and chill
  As they that lie at rest.

Yes, they are dead, yet speak
  In thunder tones unto my shrinking heart,
Driving the frozen life-blood from my cheek,
  Bidding all hope depart.

Nail down secure the coffin lid,
  Them to the deep-dug grave consign;
In the closed vaults of my heart they're hid
  Until the end of time.

Then, when the dead shall rise,
  And every secret of the heart laid bare,
I may look lovingly in their sweet eyes,
  And weep out my despair.

DESERTED.

O, FOR the joy of but one vanished hour!
O, for the heart that once was brave and strong!
Ah, me! that days of bliss should be so short,
And night of woe so long!

O, that the flowers of love should fade and die!
O, that the weeds of hate grow rank and tall!
O, that the heart must feel the sting of scorn,
Live and remember all!

If life could pass away when love shall fail!
Would death be merciful, and from us steal
The last sweet breath that can but form one name,
And all our woe conceal!

Be pitiful, Dear God! Since we must live—
My babe and I—and bear her father's name—
Give us strong hearts to hold ourselves above
The cruel, blasting shame!

Unloved? uncared for? Surely not, when He
Who hears the ravens when they cry for food,
Will care for us, His children, in our woe,
Afflicting for our good!

Out of the slag the silver, glittering, shines;
Midnight is mother of the brightest stars;
And life, which holds us with a tightening clasp
Of double prison bars,

Will one day loose us to all fond delight,
To loves and memories enduring, strong;
And death ope heaven's gates and give to us
One grand triumphal song!

A DIRGE.

Bury thy dead, faint heart!
Why clingest thou still to this unlovely clay?
The glory of thy love hath passed away,
Why not cover it deep,
Lying so calmly asleep?
Canst thou not yet with it part?

Once it was sweet, sweet heart!
Now it is cold to thee and chill,
Brought it aught to thee but ill?
Think not of days now gone,
Long hast been left alone.
Will not its memory yet depart?

Dead love to thee, proud heart!
Warm with life now to some fair, fresher face!
Once thine was full of loveliness and grace,
But hearts can change, and so
Dead love must be buried low.
Bury thy bosom's ache and smart!

No hope for thee, poor heart!
Love, once dead, is dead for evermore,
Its life no momentary madness can restore.
The form we thought so full of grace,
The beauty of the perfect face,
The glimmering glory that tipped the dart!

O love, now lost, sad heart!
O hopes, now vanished, joys now passed and gone!
O wretched waif, now doubly 'reft and lone!
Survivest thou strangely still
Through crushing grief and ill,
When youth, and love, and hope depart?

A WEDDING GIFT.

Of old, there lay one at the Temple door
Called Beautiful, and as the prophet passed
He begged an alms—for he was lame and poor,
And tears fell fast.

But Peter, fixing on him his bright eye,
Said: "Treasures of this lower earth,
Silver and gold and jewels, I have none
But what I have of worth

I freely give. Arise, and in His name,
Go forth and sing His praise!"
So, trusting in his word, he that was lame
Went happy all his days.

But thou, my little friend, when friends were few,
Who standest on the threshold of thy joy,
And seest the long way opening up for thee,
Of bliss without alloy,

What can I give to thee which thou hast not?
The kind regard of friends, when friends abound;
The love, adoring, fond, of one true heart,
With joys encompassed round.

And yet, dear girl, I dare present to thee
A gift of song, a prophecy of peace
That as thy wedded years grow ripe with age,
And married joys increase;

Thou wilt arise, and in thy richest gifts
Of womanhood, its purity and power,
Make of thy home a haven of true rest,
Wherein no storm can lower.

A WEDDING BENEDICTION

WHAT gift or guerdon sweet,
What treasure, or what sum of earthly bliss
Could equal, dear, the warm and clinging kiss
That crowns this hour so fleet?

So, if I offer naught
But words like these, though poor and weak they fall,
Know that in giving them, I give to thee
Gifts greater far than all!

Treasures of gold and gems
Are bought and sold, as neither rich nor rare;
Are meaningless as spoken sympathy,
Though light as air.

But heart's blood, coined
Into a blessing, brought and offered low,
In memory of the days of bliss which brought
But nights of woe—

Such gifts I bring thee! Then,
When others crowd around with merry words,
And thy fond heart, fill'd with o'erflowing bliss,
Is light as singing birds—

Think what may blessing cost;
And that, with laughing lip and lightsome tread
You reach one, stepping o'er the sheeted dead,
In love's grave lost!

UN FAIT ACCOMPLI.

So, 'Tis *un fait accompli*, and the ring
Is placed upon another hand than mine;
Thou'rt wedded, and life has no more to bring
To me, save memories of lost love's shrine.

The sweetest sleep that charms me from my pain,
Will bring me dreams of our commingled lot;
The wildest woe that I can ever feel
Will be to wake and find myself forgot.

A WEDDING WISH.

O, BLESSED morn in early blooming May,
That dawnest, blushing through thy cloudy veil,
Like to the bride, whose happy marriage day
Thou usherest in with soft and balmy gale.
Dost thou rejoice, thou blithely twittering bird,
And amorous woo to thee thy feathered mate?
This day a maiden speaks the solemn word
That leaves her father's house half desolate.

See! There they come—a lordly, lovely train
Of gentlemen and ladies blooming fair.
They leave the ancestral home, the church they gain,
And there before the altar kneel in prayer.

Aye, kneel and pray, thou loving, lovely one!
Much need hast thou of prayer and humble heart.
A woman's lot is on thee, and begun
This day the duty thou canst never shun
While time rolls on, until Death hurls his dart.

And while the solemn priest prays in set words,
Send thy prayers heavenward, like beauteous birds;
That never mayest thou miss the loving tone,
The kindly smile, the dark eye beaming now,
That won from thee, what is no more thine own,
Nor can be while the blood keeps onward flow.
Ah, lady, thou art young and pure and fair,
And youth and love make all things bright and sweet;
Mingle a wish in thy most fervent prayer
That Sorrow's form and thine may never meet!

O, blushing morn, that bloomest in bridal white,
Give to her eyes their most bewitching light;
Crimson her cheek and lip with tenderest flush,
That soon must kindle with a wifely blush;
Be happy, dearest, happy as the dead!
They stray, mid heaven's blest elysian bowers—
So, like them, may thy footsteps ever tread
Upon a pathway strewn with sweetest flowers.

Be happy! . May thy pure life ever be
As free from tempests, and as heavenly calm
As the still lake that lies, a trancèd mystery,
While o'er it blow spring airs of balm!

May all thy ships full-freighted to thee come,
Laden with love and joy and hope for thee;
May all good angels guard thy girlhood's home,
And love make bright the one that waiteth thee!

ALONE.

She sits alone in the fireside glow,
While the dancing shadows come and go;
And the flickering firelight's fitful gleam
Seems like the ghost of a vanished dream.

What a dream was that, her pure, sweet soul
Saw in the light of the glowing coal
Once, so long ago, of a perfect life
And a happiness rare, to be *his* wife!

She had bowed her head with a maiden shame,
As she thought how sweet to be called by his name;
To be sheltered for aye in his heart's strong love,
Was a joy only second to heaven above.

What a picture of bliss her fancy made,
While the gleaming firelight dancing, played
O'er her broad, high brow, and plain brown hair,
As she wondered how he had found her fair.

Not beautiful she, nor wise, nor good,
With a dash of temper, a fitful mood,
(Born of her dreamy poet's heart)—
No matter, he loved her,—they could not part.

They would meet life's shadows, side by side;
And the morn was fair that made her his bride;
But the clouds came fast, and the old wives said
'Twould be better for her if she had not wed.

That was almost two years ago;
And to-night she sits in the gleam and glow
Of her hearth alone, and sighs with regret
For the sound of a footstep that comes not yet.

Her husband is absent night after night;
She has failed to make his hearthstone bright.
Is marriage a failure? she feels, alas!
Only a loss of love could bring it to pass.

GREETING TO CLEVELAND.

A NEW State in the Union! Let me see!
An annexation, that means anarchy,
For when a man is married, he's in doubt
Whether he's master in the house or out;
And when a woman weds she's just as sure
That she must hold the reins firm and secure.
You'll find more trouble, Cleveland, and dismay,
Than if you had annexed fair Canada,
With the Dominion Government thrown in,
And C. P. R., with loads of debt and sin;
With Costigan and Blake full of Home Rule,
O'Donohue, of whom they made a tool
To get the Catholic vote; and heaps of people
With pride (not power), like a church steeple.
But annexation and home rule to the fore,
With Goldwin Smith, and—Respectfully,

MAUDE MOORE.

HE COMES NOT YET.

Is that his step upon the gravel walk ?
Is it his shadow which the bright moon throws
Across the dew-bright grass ? Is it his breath
That greets me, or the perfume of the rose ?
Alas ! he comes not yet !

Did he not call me ? surely his soft voice
Sounded with love's own accent in my ear,
As oft before it came upon my heart,
Soothing alarm, and banishing vain fear ;
Ah ! no, he comes not yet.

My heart will hear him ere my sluggish sense
Can sift the meaning of its quickened beat.
My heart will bud and blossom as the rose,
Though every fibre falter 'neath his feet.
But oh ! he comes not yet !

ROSEMARY.

"There's rosemary. That's for remembrance."

I GIVE thee a leaf. 'Tis a simple thing,
But it may, perchance, to your memory bring
A thought of the happy days gone by,
When care had not clouded your sunny eye.

Keep it ! When friends prove false and cold,
When life is withered and time grown old,
Still may this leaf be unto thee
A type of unfading constancy.

Green and fresh may it ever remain,
The same as now newly washed by rain;
So may the memory of ——— seem
Like the lingering light of a witching dream.

'Twas a wild, sweet dream that once swayed our hearts,
The remembrance of which not soon departs;
But we severed each tie and the dream is gone,
Though the light it once shed still shineth on.

MY BOY FROM THE BANKS OF ANNAN.

Of all the lads in east or west,
For blessin' or for bannin',
I dearly lo'e my Jam the best,—
My boy from the banks of Annan.

Sae sloe-black is his wavy hair,
Sae saft his e'en o' gray,
Sae douce and bonnie a' his air,
He's stown my heart away.

Yet oh, he is an unco' chiel,
For spite of all my airt,
There's aye anither has the fiel',
Anither lass his heart.

Yet oft he swore he dearly lo'ed
Nane but his bonnie Bess,
Sae, though some say he's fause to me,
I'll lo'e him nane the less.

Sae, Jeanie, cease your flirting ways;
I'll gie ye muckle thanks,
Gin ye will cease his flame to raise,
My boy from Annan's banks.

Ye may ha'e all the bonnie e'en
That flash frae honour's ranks,
Gin ye gif o'er my humble clerk,
My boy from Annan's banks.

ALBUM VERSES.

TO ALICE.

SWEET Alice, in life's dewy morn,
When hearts are young, and love is warm,
Poets may sing in melting lays
Of youth, and love, and joyous days.

There's naught so fair as young love's dream,
There's naught so swift as life's gay stream,
There's naught so sweet as wedded bliss,
There's naught so pure as love's first kiss.

And yet, dear girl, in after years,
When sadly fall slow-dropping tears,
We mourn the youth now fled and gone,
And fear old age that's creeping on.

Our hearts are warm, though blood is slow,
Eyes bright, though cheeks have lost their glow,
And hearts are young though locks are gray,
And life is sweet, though past its May.

We've learned the lesson taught by years,
That skies, though bright, may yet shed tears,
Though truth, and love, and hope be given,
There's nothing real but God and Heaven!

TO MARY.

MAIDEN, with the sweetest name
  Ever yet to woman given,
Seest thou up that shining pathway,
  Through earth's clouds and sorrows riven?
Dost thou mark those other Marys
  Who have trod the way before?
Art thou treading in their footsteps,
  Till they greet thee at the door?

Maiden, with the name immortal,
  (Sweeter poet never sung);
Never yet were sweeter accents
  Syllabled by lover's tongue;
Mayst thou ever be as now,
  Happy, fair and free from guile,
Laying up that lore of love
  That winneth Heaven's warmest smile.

I, alas! am that lone other,
  "Cumbered o'er with many cares,"
Dragging out my strange existence
  'Mid life's heavy toils and snares.
But I trust, aye, *trust I only?*
  That at last we two shall meet,
Where we sweet shall sing together
  Sitting at the Saviour's feet.

To the City's shining portals,
  The "gate Beautiful" I go;
Though I may be weak and sinful,
  I shall enter there, I know.
Where the long cool grass and flowers,
  Wave in shady places deep,
When I, like a child fault-chidden,
  Sob myself at last to sleep.

WAITING.

ALL things may come by waiting, so I wait
  And list thy footfall on the silent walk;
The night wind moans with many voices! Hushed
  Are sounds of laughter and of cheerful talk.

The lights go out, and one by one the stars
  Look down upon me with enquiring eye;
O! love, they mark but carking care's caress,
  As lone I wait in tearless agony.

SABBATH CHIMES.

SOFTLY stealing through the air,
  Sabbath chimes so sweetly come,
Calling to the house of prayer
  Where the wretched find a home.

Where the weary find a rest,
  Where the worn may be at peace,
Leaning on the Saviour's breast,
  All their toils and cares may cease.

Church and creed alike forgot,
God's own children are ye all ;
Rich and poor, whate'er your lot,
Hasten at the Sabbath's call.

Sabbath chimes, how sweet the sound,
Cleaving earthly stillness vast
In the blue cerulean dome,
Endeth now in joy at last !

LADY MAUDE.

I SIT in my spacious chamber,
And watch the ruddy light,
Cast on the walls and alcoves,
From the glowing anthracite ;
And I lean my head, with its curls of gold,
Upon my jewelled hand;
"The fairest lady in all the court,
The richest in all the land."

So say the suitor lordlings
That throng within my train,
And the beauty and wealth of Lady Maude
Is toasted again and again.
I brightly smile and turn awhile
From the crowded, blazing hall,
To where the light of a taper bright
Breaks through the night's dark pall.

Within, by its single glimmer,
Sits a maiden young and fair,
With cheeks like crimson cherries,
And wealth of raven hair.

A lover lies with half-closed eyes
  Upon the mat at her feet,
And gazes oft, with loving glance,
  Upon his mistress sweet.

And what have I, the Lady Maude,
  The proud and courted dame,
To do with this home-scene of bliss
  In this hut without a name?
I reign a queen, right royal, I ween,
  Over all the titled throng;
She owneth only one subject leal,
  She reigneth in one heart alone.

THE RECALL.

Come home to the heart of thy mother, my boy,
  That never will change or grow cold;
To the arms that first cradled thee, eldest born joy,
  Thy mother grows weary and old.
'Twas a bright July day, in the long, long ago,
  When I found you asleep on my breast;
And I held to my heart the first-born of my house,
  With a feeling of exquisite rest.

Many and strange are the changes that come
  To the hearts of humanity here,
But the heart of a mother is always the same,
  And her children are evermore dear.
Though trust waxes old, and affection grows cold
  In the heart of the once-cherished wife,
Enshrined is the child in the strong mother love,
  Which but deepens and broadens through life.

TO G. A R.,

Of old, an aged and impotent man
  Lay by Bethesda's famous healing spring,
Waiting the hour, weary and worn, when
  A splendid Angel with a silver wing,
Should stir its solemn depths and bring to light
  The healing virtues which therein abode;
But heartsore and discouraged, for each time,
  Another got before him in the road.

Just so, my distant, unknown, German friend,
  I must await the angel of my verse;
I cannot write a poem at my will,
  Else your epistle might be anwered worse;
'T is bad enough as 't is—but you perceive,
  My muse is chary of caressing;
Not wishing to be rude, I take my leave,
  Leaving my autograph and blessing.

Gallipolis, O.

MOTHERHOOD.

God's gracious, perfect gift to womankind
Lies in the compass of this simple word.
Through weary weeks we wait, and watch, and hope,
And weave sweet fancies of the bright to-be,
When, after toil and trouble, woe and pain,
We hold within the circle of our arms
That which makes life worth living, joy more sweet,
And toil and pain but empty wordings framed

By those who miss from out their selfish lives,
Children's sweet laughing lips and love-lit eyes,
Sent fresh from Heaven to gladden hearthstones here.
My babe, my blessing! my sweet blue-eyed girl!
My week-old darling! June's most perfect rose!

* * * * * *

So wrote I, more than a decade agone,
And now she stands my tender little bud,
Just on the eve of bursting into bloom
Of gracious womanhood. My rose of roses,
My little girl just entering her teens!
May the good God go with thee, precious child,
So that, when after years bring bloom from bud,
And choice fulfilment of long-cherished hope,
I may give back to Him who gave it me,
The fair page of thy life, unstained by blot,
And rich with pure and holy thought,—a leaf
Fit for perusal by the Holy Eye
To whom our lives are as an open book.
This from her mother, with a mother's love.

June 25th, 1877.

THE SNOW.

FLOATETH the fleecy, fast-falling snow
From the dim grey sky to the earth below,
Enveloping hamlet, and hill, and wold
With an ermine mantle, white and cold.
And Lake Ontario's blue, cold waves
Sighing and singing o'er deep-dug graves,
Are shut from our sight by a wall of white;
And I sit and dream, in the leaden light,

Of a land that lies beneath warmer skies,
Where the sultry summer never dies;
Of a Southern land, where with anthem grand,
The silver sea laves the golden sand;
Of its days of calm, and its nights of balm,
And waving foliage of pine and palm.
But my dream dies away, and the light of day
Fades into the gloaming, cold and gray,
And the beautiful snow to the earth below
Floateth and singeth a song so low,
That unless you possess an exquisite ear,
Its low-toned notes you will scarcely hear.
But this is the song that it singeth so sweet,
While thousands are treading it under their feet.

"I come from above
On a mission of love,
To teach you a lesson taught with great rarity;
With my flaky wings
I cover all things,
And throw over all my mantle of charity.

For though I am pure,
And from sin secure,
I bow to the sinful in all humility;
I quietly fall,
And cover them all—
I treat rich and poor alike with civility.

I love to cover
The cold ground over,
And leave all the color, and warmth, and glow,
And the last summer's bloom,
In darksome tomb,
Down in the depths of the dead earth below.

They are fettered fast
In my arms at last,
And I hold them warmly, yet with all purity,
But when spring shall come,
From their wintry tomb
They will glide forth gladly in all security.

There are those who sleep
In their graves down deep,
And their marble houses I've coated over,
But they never will know
If they lie beneath snow,
Or under bright mantles of blossoming clover."

This is the song, as it floateth along,
That the snow sings to me this Sabbath night;
And I dream no more of a far-off shore,
But turn to the fire's ruddy light.
And while the fire leaps high and higher,
I thank our Father for glorious life,
And my glad heart sings that the future brings
Long, happy days, free from care and strife.

NEW YEAR SONG.

A WILD, wet night!
The snow lies piled in heavy heaps;
The wind wails wild and never sleeps;
A dark, drear night!

The coming year
Is ushered in with storm and sleet,
Which clouds the lamps along the street,
Making all drear.

A year ago
My heart beat high with hope and glee,
For friends I loved encompassed me,
Friends now laid low!

Low in their graves
Lie those I loved a year ago;
Above them pelt the sleet and snow,
And the wind raves.

Blest be the dead!
They stray 'mid heaven's happy bowers,
While glide along earth's wintry hours
With weary tread.

All hail the year!
In storm or sunshine, wind or calm,
In joy or sorrow, grief or balm,
Give him good cheer!

OLD YEAR GOOD-BYE.

Soft lies the snow on the moor and the mountain,
Cold hangs the moon in yon clear winter sky,
Bright gleam her rays on yon frozen fountain,
Nature proclaims that the old year must die.
Old year, good-bye!
Since you must die.
Sweet be your sleep in the grave of the past;
Old friends must part,
However the heart
In its fond grief to the loved form clings fast.

Here in the twilight sadly I ponder
On hopes that beamed bright in the days of your youth.
How lightly and gayly the moments we squander !
While time is yet young we believe in man's truth !
Old year, good-bye !
Since you must die,
You gave me good friends and true ;
They are parted from me
By land and by sea ;
And now I must part, too, from you.

The gold-gleaming gates of the past are closed on you,
The dim distance veils our fond friends from our eyes;
Still, we cherish you both, and ever think on you,
Though your forms never more on our vision may rise.
Dear friends, good-bye !
New Year is nigh !
Though we may grieve for the friends we have lost,
Still, life must go on
Till, the prizes all won,
We regret not the tears or the labor they cost.

THE DYING YEAR.

A TRUSTED friend, a tried and true,
Is stricken down to death ;
Gather around and catch the words
That come with his latest breath.

Tread softly round his snow-draped couch,
His head lies low at last ;
His breath comes quick and cold, e'en now
His voice is failing fast.

Bend low, and listen eagerly,
His counsel now implore;
Make haste, come quickly, for I hear
A footfall at the door.

The hour grows late. He'll soon be gone,
A stranger will be here;
The old man gives us to his son,
The new and untried year.

The clock is nearly on the stroke,
Alas! the wintry night
Is rounding to its noon! He'll not
Be here to see the light.

Ah, think not that the coming year
Will be as tried and true,
As this, that you exchange for him,
The old friend for the new.

Ye waste the wealth of love to throw
Thus idly from you away
The friend that was your good old friend,
For the new one of to-day.

Call back the breath that fleeteth fast,
Call back the dying year!
Vain are our fond regrets and prayers,
He cannot see or hear.

But hark! Our old friend speaketh now,
List we the words he saith:
"Give him the love ye gave to me,
I give him birth in my death."

He's gone! draw soft the shrouding sheet,
  Above the face so dear;
Step from the couch and greet the son,
  All hail to the New Year!

CHRISTMAS BELLS.

O, Christmas bells, sing loud and clear!
  Make liquid music o'er the earth;
You bring to all peace and good cheer;
  Ring in, clear bells, the Christ-child's birth.

O, merry bells of Yule! ye tell
  Of love and joys due unto each;
Joys loud in every clanging swell,
  Love wide around as space can reach.

This is the poor man's day of joy,
  The day of thanks and jubilee!
He takes his babe, a black-eyed boy,
  And seats him proudly on his knee.

He looks upon his faithful wife
  Through eyes half-blind with happy tears,
And thanks his God for glorious life,
  And this dear partner of his years.

Peace upon earth! Good will to men!
  He softly chants the angels' song,
And from his narrow window then
  Looks out upon the passing throng.

Some go to revel, some to prayer;
  Some wear gay robes and faces bright;
Some bring to the cold winter air,
  Thin rags and features pinched and white.

Ring on, blithe bells! 'Tis life and love,
  'Tis saving grace to rich and poor;
Both bend alike to God above,
  Both enter in at heaven's one door!

A NEW YEAR DREAM.

I FELL asleep just as the softening chimes
Announced that clanging bells had ceased to ring
The old and dead year to the dim, dark past,
And ushered in the glad and happy year,
That seemed to some so full of precious things—
And some more dark and dreary than the dead.
To me, the last thought of my waking hour
Was, what more precious and more joyous gift
Could this new friend, whom yet I knew not, bring
Unto my life than the old to me had given;
And what wish would I have that I had not.
So waking dreamed I, and so sleeping dreamed.

Methought, within the shadows dim and dewy
Of an old wood I wandered far and long;
'Twas spring, and sovereign nature had put on
Her freshest robes of tender green; and song
From myriad-throated warblers made the cool
And cloistered copse delirious with delight.
A lazy frog sat, round-eyed, near a pool
That made its bed by moss half hid from sight;

And all my being thrilled with happiness,
And that tumultuous throbbing of the breast
Which comes but when the tides of youth and spring
Make fancies, bird-like, mount on airy wing.

Then lying on the lush-green grass, I seemed
To feel a presence other than my own,
And, turning, saw a form of majesty—
And face which with an awful grandeur shone.
Then to me, trembling, spoke this presence high :
" Mortal, thy heart I read, yet fain would see
What thou would'st choose for this, thy New Year's
gift,
If thou could'st have thy choice of things to be ;
Would'st wealth, or fame, or love ? For without one
Of these, thy life is surely lived in vain.
Search thy soul diligently that thou may'st
Choose wisely, shunning future care and pain."
Then, quieting my trembling heart, I spoke :
" Angel, for such I deem thee, bright and fair,
Pray show to me the virtues of each gift
That, having knowledge, I may my choice declare."

The angel smiled, and then, a shifting scene!
I saw myself with luxury and ease
Surrounded. All that money could devise—
In richest raiment clothed, with dainties served,
With overflowing purse to feed the poor ;
With all the splendour of magnificence
I saw myself surrounded, but alone !
" Wilt thou have wealth ?" the angel asked. I smiled
And shook my head. The picture lacked somewhat ;
I hardly knew what else I wanted there,
But let the picture pass away from sight.
And then there came before my dazzled eyes

That vision dearest to the poet's soul—
Upon a background of high mountains, white
With everlasting snow and glittering ice,
Emblem of pure and spotless fame, I saw
The flame-emblazoned scroll; and writ thereon,
Among the proud and lofty names of those
Who have made bright and better all the earth,
In that they lived therein, and toiled, and sung;
And, pictured there, in proud pre-eminence,
My name among the foremost ones of earth,
My form among the noblest of earth's sons.
My longing eyes looked vainly on the crowd
Of upturned faces, my companions there,
Something about the picture broke the charm;
I turned away from the bright scene, and sighed.
"Wilt thou have Fame?" the Angel gently asked.
And slowly, tearfully, I answered, "No!"

And then there broke on my enraptured sight
A picture sweet, of such supreme delight!
A quiet lane bordered with gnarled old trees,
Which led up to a quaint old garden, where,
Sitting so carelessly content, upon
The threshhold of an ivy-hung old house,
Two figures, side by side, the picture showed—
Two rosy children sported at their feet;
The peaceful cows grazed in the field near by,
The sheep with snowy fleece lay on the slope;
The hum of murmurous insects filled the air,
And bright-hued birds flitted among the trees,
Filling with sweetest song the summer sky.
From the barnyard crowed chanticleer in joy
The mother-hen marshalled her fluffy chicks
Before her, with sedate and stately step.

I looked upon the figures in the porch,
One was my own, and, touched with sudden thought,
I turned me to the angel at my side.
"Wilt thou have Love?" the Angel softly asked.
"Sweet Angel," prayed I, "show me but the face
Companion to my own!" "Dost thou not know?"
I looked, I cried: "I will take only love!"
The face was thine! I woke! the dream was o'er.

So though the New Year hold for me nor wealth,
Nor fame, the brilliant meteor of a day,
I know that thou wilt love me, aye for aye,
And with that knowledge, I defy all else.

A WINTER NIGHT.

Over all the winter, starlight icily is falling;
Over all the snow, a great white cloak is softly lying;
While from all its covering close, the buds and flowers are calling,
And the tall and dusky pine trees with voices sad are sighing.

Wild and weary howls the wind through lone woodland passes;
The leafless boughs of forest trees sway tossing in its might;
The snow lies piled on window-ledge in huge, mis-shapen masses;
And falls the glittering starlight over all the solemn night.

Midwinter nights in moonless skies and northern scenes are cheerless,
Though beauty bend from every flashing star its radiance bright;
The moon must walk in majesty and might, the queen, the peerless,
Else give me the glowing fire in place of northern night.

The glowing fire, the sparkling fire, flying up the flue broad-throated,
While my trusty dog lies at my feet, my trusted friend sits near;
And I envy not the sleigh-rider, fur-muffled and great-coated,
Though winter be the carnival of all the glorious year.

Home joys are sweetest. O, ye maids and bachelors now listen!
Home ties, home loves are dearer than all other joys [beside.
Let the stars shine down on happy hearts, and on the pure snow glisten,
While I sit beside my happy hearth, no want nor woe betide!

A VALENTINE.

I WALKED along the street one day,
Not many weeks ago,
And met a glance from two blue eyes
That set my cheeks aglow.
And since that time, by day or night,
My heart was robbed of rest,
Nor lay secure as heretofore
Within its peaceful nest.

Those eyes have haunted all my dreams;
  In dreams that moustached lip
Is pressed against my own, as bees
  From flowers honey sip;
In dreams those arms have clasped me close,
  That voice has whispered "Mine!"
So that I cannot rest until
  I pray St. Valentine.

" O, good and kindly saint, to whom
  All woful maidens pray,
Unbend the heart of this proud man;
  Give him no rest by day,
No sleep by night, no loving arms,
  No loving heart's repose,
Till he shall see that with but me
  Must all his wooings close!

May all his wandering thoughts depart,
  All dreams of others flee,
So that his blue eyes see but one,
  And may that one be me!
Do this, good saint, and evermore
  Upon thy votive shrine,
I'll lay the tribute of my verse,
  O, good St. Valentine!

And, if he read this simple rhyme,
  As he so surely may,
He'll know at once who wrote it
  And come to me and say:
'This is the day made sacred
  To love and all its charms,
And so I come to you, my dear,
  To quiet your alarms.

You'll know by this, my first love-kiss,
  There is no surer sign,
That for all time I pledge myself
  Your faithful Valentine!'"

STANDING IN THE SNOW.

TARRY awhile, my lady,
  'Tis a cold, cold winter's night.
Look abroad on the starry sky,
  And the dead earth robed in white.

Go back to the fire, my lady!
  Shutters and curtains close.
Sit 'neath the glare of your brilliant light,
  Fresh as the heart of a rose.

Think of the poor, my lady,
  The beggars that pass your gate.
See where they stand with outstretched hand—
  Stand at your door and wait.

Though you may care, my lady,
  I hope you may never know
How the cold chills to the heart of those
  Who stand with their feet in the snow.

Humanity poor, my lady!
  Made in the image of God,
Whether they sleep in downy beds,
  Or on the snow-covered sod.

Do not forget, my lady,
Riches may take to them wings!
But a free heart and a generous hand
Much joy to the giver brings.

Sit by the fire, my lady,
And bask in its ruddy glow!
But do not forget the many that wait
And, shivering, stand in the snow!

PROMISE.

Sweep softly, Spring!
On balmy wing,
With gentle streamlets murmuring;
With dreamful eyes
I watch the skies,
And breathe the airs of Paradise.

The light winds sigh,
And through the sky
The light, white clouds skim softly by;
I watch them sail
Borne by the gale,
Far, far away, till sight they fail.

From upland, lea,
And maple tree,
The gleam of green comes glowingly,
And through the wood
Blossom and bud
Start forth afresh from wintry shroud.

O! soft spring air,
A message bear
To her, the fairest of the fair;
In love-tones low,
Then whisper how
On Hope's fair tree the blossomed bough

Hangs low; and soon,
'Neath reddening noon,
And coming summer's softened croon,
With fruitage rife
Will glow with life,
And crown thee, darling, happy wife!

O! joy to be,
That comes to thee
So dreamfully and tenderly!
Break into bowers
Of bridal flowers,
And bring the best of happy hours!

DETHRONED.

O! GRIM ice-king, dethroned at last!
Too long thou reigned'st o'er the earth,
With rudest storm and chilliest blast,
Destroying all our joy and mirth.

Thou stand'st at bay, an uncrowned king,—
Thy throne an ice-berg toppling down,
Thy sceptre but a worthless thing,
And on thy head a melting crown.

Thou seest thine earthly glories fade,
As many a king before has done,—
With flashing eye and icy beard,
Thou seest thy race is almost run.

Dost see thy rival? fair and young,
With gentle eye and modest mien;
Trailing her virgin robes along,
She cometh, clad in gleaming green.

Looks she a formidable foe?
Thou laugh'st in scorn, though lying low.
One single blast of thy rude breath
Would crush her 'neath a whirl of snow.

But thou, oh King, hast yet to learn
That not in strength lieth greatest guile,
That many a brow, though thunder-clothed,
May brighten 'neath a woman's smile.

That many an arm though hard and strong,
And heart, though stoutest in the land,
Groweth pliant as a leathern thong
Beneath a woman's wielding hand.

It is no shame to thee to know
Thy throne usurped by such a one,
Though on her royal head she wears
A rosy, not an icy crown.

Yield up thy frost-gemmed sceptre, king!
Put off thy robe of ermine white!
Our Queen a flower-wreathed wand doth bring,
Her face is fairer to our sight.

Lie low, expire without a groan,
  Tears come amiss in time of mirth;
Queen Spring, a maiden fair and young,
  Reigneth triumphant o'er the earth,

AN EASTER OFFERING.

An Easter offering? Nay, friend of mine,
What gift can honor Him who gave me thee,
For whom all else of earth I would resign?
Thus, having gold, who would wish dross to see?
But 'tis thy dear request; and as thy will
In all things worketh to the mastery,
Even to commanding all my heart and brain,
And, as it now is, evermore must be.

*   *   *   *

'Twas night in old Judea, long ago,
And darkness, deep and heavy, hovered o'er
The earth, bowed down by weight of infamy,
And at Christ's crucifixion stricken sore
With heavy presages, thick hung the air,
Stirred sluggishly as by a mourner's sigh;
But soon a balmy southern breeze upsprang
And freed from cloud and gloom the bright'ning sky,
As dawned the new-born day with ecstacy
Of babbling stream fresh loosed from wintry thrall,
And late-dropped dew on leaf and blade of grass,
And early waking bird with timid call.
And then uprose the royal king of day,

And, from his thronèd sphere, cast golden rays
In myriad eyes reflected brilliantly,
Glinting the garments sad of Mary Magdalen,
Hasting with heavy heart once more to gaze
On the dead features of the King of men!
Ah, what sad thoughts! He whom her heart received,
And worshipped as her Saviour lay within,
Puissant, no more! He whose word alone
Had cleansed her pure from all her secret sins.
But her fond woman's heart, so full of woe,
Must sacrifice of sweet spices make
Against His burial. Her hopes, her love,
Her deep devotion must this comfort take.
"He savèd others," they had mocking said,
"Himself he cannot save," and her poor heart
Lay bleeding beside her Master's lifeless clay,
Powerless laid by death's cruel dart.
She had not heard the rushing sound that cleaved
Through the thick clouds, and seen her Lord received
Into His Father's arms as He ascended,
And all the glory that thereon attended.
The night, to her o'erburdened with woes,
Had been long, dark and sorrowful. E'en the sun
As with unwonted, threefold splendor rose,
As if the jubilee of worlds began
This blessed morn, had failed to dissipate
The direful clouds of deep and dark despair
That hovered o'er her soul's horizon. Fate
Had filled with heaviest omens all the air.

But, as with faltering step she seeks the tomb,
Even her sweet sacrifices seem denied;
He's gone! In vain she peers into the gloom.
At last one sitting near she has descried,

In shining garb, the glory of whose guise
She has not noted, for she, tearful, cries:
"Where have ye laid Him? Tell me!"
Anguish keen
Pictured in her pale face and streaming eyes.
Then, as he answers her in joyful strain:
"He is not here, but risen, *as He said!*"
She knows him angel. Oh, the sudden joy
Of doubt dispelled and doomed forever dead,
And faith renewed forever to abide,
And hope, new-wakened, thought forever fled,
And love, once lost, regained and purified!
"He is not dead, but risen, as He said!"

She flies on wingèd feet of joy and love,
To tell the tidings to each one she meets;
And as the joyful strain she chants again,
And all the wondrous story she repeats,
Angels take up the song that men have sung,
And throughout earth, and far in heaven above,
The chorus swells: "The Lord is risen again.
The Lord is risen, the world is saved by love!"

* * * *

Fair is this Easter morn, without a trace
Of cloud or care careering o'er its face;
And shining Easter lilies bud and bloom,
To gladden our remembrance of the tomb
That gave so glorious a gift to-day,
That men and angels may rejoice alway.
Father of mercies! to Thy throne we lift
Our hearts to-day for Thy most precious gift,
Thine only Son! sacrificed for our need.
Joyful we sing, "The Lord is risen indeed!"

Help us to bury in His empty grave
All our dark sins, our follies that deprave,
Our littleness, and pride, and self-conceit,
Give Thou the grace to tread them 'neath our feet,
That with joy, hope and love all newly-born,
We grateful rise on this glad Easter morn.

The night is past, and yet the long, dark night
Makes tenfold dearer the sweet morning light.
So, dearer thou, for faults lived down, to me,
And love, new-shining as the morn shall be;
The dear old love, that seems yet pure and new,
When clouds of doubt dispel and bring to view
All the long-buried joys of other days,
Brightened tenfold by these returning rays
Of that glad day, when souls in sin's dark prison,
Break forth and sing: "The Lord indeed is risen!"

We praise Thee for the blessings shed around,
The place whereon we stand is holy ground.
Beneath our feet are buried all our woes,
And all that e'er disturbed our heart's repose;
Jesus of Nazareth! Thy open tomb
Holds treasures for which earth can find no room.
Thy Cross gleams white against a sun-bright sky,
A ladder by which we may climb on high.
While men may chant, while angels sing above:
"The Lord is risen! The world is saved by love!"

Love, beautiful, immortal, perfect, true,
Love, powerful all evil to subdue,
Love that alone all mortals good can bring,
The gift of Thee, our risen Lord and King!

AN APRIL EVE.

I THANK thee, Heaven! a lovely April eve,
After an April day of smiles and tears,
I, sitting at my chamber window here,
Which, facing southward, overlooks the street,
And, past the piles of brick and mortar, leads
The vision to the steel-blue lake beyond,
With quiet farms and cottages between.
Far fleeting clouds, half purple and half gray,
Like scattered ashes, dead, and dull and drear,
The sun has left behind him in his wake,
To mourn the dying of the sweet spring day.
The airs that steal about me are replete
With living sweetness. Slowly now descends,
With loving lingering, twilight, gray and damp;
Gently and quietly the lighter shades
Commingle with the darker, till deep night
Encompasses each object round about
With murky and mysterious silences.

A LITTLE GRAVE.

SOME mother's treasure lies buried below
Under the cold silent clod;
Some mother's teardrops unceasingly flow
For the little one "Gone to its God."

Some mother kneels by this three feet of earth,
O'er which the willows wave;
Some mother prays for the glorious new birth,
Over this grassy grave.

O, a little grave hath a hold in the heart,
  And a tale will sadly tell
Of one who on earth for a time held part,
  Then fled where Cherubim dwell.

A little place vacant at bed and board,
  A cradle song unsung;
A memory sweet in the heart snugly stored
  Of the darling who died so young.

And is this all? Will the solemn night
  That broods o'er the mother's way,
Be dispersed by the faint gray dawn of light
  Deepening full to the perfect day?

Will the shadows hovering about her heart
  Be chased away by joy?
Be patient, mother! who threw the dart
  Can care the best for thy boy!

DEDICATION.

"Poet, what of the night?"
  Ah, child, it is long!
  It cometh in sighing and sorrow.
  It giveth no promise of morrow.
  It passeth in darkness and tears,
  In longings, and hopings, and fears;
  And then, without any warning,
  Like a nymph from the wave arising,
  Our eyes with her beauty surprising,
  It breaketh to gladness of morning—
  A morning of sunshine and song!
  'Tis worth all the darkness and gloom,

The waiting and watching for light,
The sorrow that shrouded the night,
These hopes that arise from the tomb,
Where they in their ashes were laid,
Their pride and their beauty decayed.

"But the morning, the glorious morning,
Every leaf, shrub, and flower adorning,
Begemmed and bejewelled with dew,—
Can it ever love's sweetness renew?"

Ah, but the night has been long!
The rosy god loves light and song.
He heareth not sighing and sorrow,
His wings all their swiftest plumes borrow
To waft him to a happier sphere,
Where flowers bloom brightly all the year,
Where darkness and despair are not,
Where grief's grim form will be forgot;
While all the tears that e'er perplexed him,
And all the frowns that ever vexed him,
He buries in another's arms,
And quite forgets poor Psyche's charms.
Ah, yes, the night is too long!
And alas there is no returning
Of love in the brightness of morning,
The morning of sunshine and song!

"But the poet's poor heart throbs with pleasure,
As he warbles an exquisite measure,—"
Telling the listening throng
A tale of trouble and wrong,
Of sorrow and darkness lived over,
Of shadow and night passed away,
Of clouds on his soul's sky that hover,
Spirit wounds he tries vainly to cover,

With talk of the bee on the clover,
The daisy, the bird on her nest,
The summer-cloud yet in the west;
How from the calm lake laughs the loon
In the sunshine of radiant June,
In the beauty and glory of day.
The gall that was poured in his wine
Only maks the soul's music more fine.
This, then, is his mission in life,
To be the sweet note in the strife,
The tone that remains with the heart,
When the harsher notes quickly depart.

Ah, Dear! though you cannot be dearer,
Nor in this world can ever come nearer,
There is no resurrection for love!
When once he hath lain in the grave,
Or sunk 'neath adversity's wave,
He hath no other life left above!

THE OLD MAN FOR HIS YOUNG WIFE DEAD.

HOLD me close in thy fond, loving arms,
Mother earth.
In thine ever-extended strong arms!
I have trod on thy bosom full many a year;
I have laughed joy's loud laugh, and have wept sorrow's tear;
I have seen friends and loved ones laid in thy embrace,
And the dread coffin-lid covered over a face
Bedight with youth's loveliest charms, mother earth,
The type of all beauty and worth!

I want to lie down by her side, Mother Earth,—
To lie down by the side of my bride!
Thy face has lost all its first freshness to me;
No wanton wind playing o'er woodland and lea,
No bird warbling sweetly, no flower blooming fair,
No sweet sounds of summer to me pleasing are
When the face of my darling's denied, Mother Earth!
And the eyes that beamed bright at my hearth.

Fold us both in the warmth of thy breast, Mother Earth,
Both together, there calm let us rest!
Give to them that would ask, every good thing of life,
So they take without wishing its hardship and strife;
But to us,—give us peace like a lake in a calm;
Let winter snow wrap us, or summer's sweet balm,
We will be in our bridal robes drest, Mother Earth!
And be born of the Heavenly birth!

A REVERIE.

I STOOD within a city of the dead,
  And marked its marble monuments and towers,
Pacing the silent streets with stealthy tread,
  Wearying with tears the sad, sweet summer hours.

Over the grass-green mound hummed the wild bee,
  Laden with honey, homeward bound;
The lake lay far below, a trancèd mystery,
  Solemn, and calm and white, by a blue belt sphered round!
A speck upon its surface floated far,
  I knew it for a ship, bound for that shore,
Where I do long to stand, and make or mar
  My fortune in the world's rude selfish roar.

*   *   *   *   *

Ambition here among these silent graves?
  Thou bane of life, O, let me bow my head!
Why can I not forget this voice that raves
  Of fame and wealth, even here, among the dead?

In vain, in vain! I must yield even love,
  Without which, what is life? For this mere breath.
This puff of cloud upon a sunset sky,—
  Only to win a name that defies death!

The cooing doves below bring back to me
  What I have vowed forever to forget.
Ah, love, by force alone I yielded thee,—
  Not force of my own will—with eyelids wet.

Well, thou art gone, and cold to me and still
  As those who silent lie beneath this sod,
Courage, faint heart? Some day thou too shalt rest
  And scorn may then ride over thee roughshod.

IN LATE OCTOBER.

Liest thou there so lowly,
    Poor dead earth of mine,
'Reft of thy summer's glory,
'Reft of thy song and sunshine,
    Faded the flowers,
    Blasted the bowers.
Chill winds have withered and left thee to pine;
  Song birds are fled,
  Joy lieth dead,
Where is thy grandeur, poor Earth of mine?

Earth made reply :
Mortal, thine eye,
Can it not see where the red Autumn gleams ?
Canst thou not see,
Enveloping me,
Ember-like leaflets through which beauty beams ?
Over my breast,
Lying at rest,
Hovers the haze which the Autumn sun spreads ;
Like the veil of the bride,
Which doth cover, not hide
Her beauty and grace from the loved one she weds.

Winter is coming to wed me !
Hast thou not seen
Frost's silver sheen,
The messenger he has sped me,
Bringing a glittering crown for a Queen.
I will not sigh,
Joy draweth nigh,
Splendor most regal and pomp half-divine !
Soon thou'lt rejoice
At the Frost-king's voice,
And pity no longer, "poor Earth of mine!"

A MEMORY OF NOVEMBER.

THE night's baith murk and cauld, Willie,
Nae blinkin' stars shine oot;
The win' sweeps by wi' mournfu' tone,
And blaws the leaves aboot.
The last day o' November, Willie !
Ah ! weel I ken the time ;
'Twas thretty autumns o' lang syne,
And we were in our prime.

I made a bonnie bride, ye said ;
And ne'er a lad was there,
In a' the town or countrie roun'
That wi' ye could compare !
Y'er sloe-black eyes and jetty hair,
Y'er cheek a ruddy hue,
Nae lad was there in a' the town
I wad ha'e ta'en for you.

We're growin' auld, my bonnie Will !
Ye'r locks are siller white ;
Ye'r cheeks ha'e lost their ruddy glow,
Ye'r e'en their sparkle bright.
I, too, am faded ; but the luve
That in our hearts did glow,
Burns yet wi' just as fierce a flame
As thretty years ago !

COURAGE.

THE other night,
When the wind blew the blinding snow and sleet,
Building in air a winding wall of white,
And blanketing the street,

A little bird,
A wayward wanderer of the upper air,
Came to my window making itself heard,
Wishing an entrance there.

With wing and bill,
And tiny, trembling, restless, clutching feet,
Essayed to find a vulnerable point,
Beat and returned to beat.

And then I oped
The window wide and wooed the wanderer near,
And the tired bird, in gaining all it hoped,
Began to fear.

And, with quick wing
It sought the darkest corner of the room,
And safety found in trembling cowering
Within the gloom.

And then I thought
How often, when we covet some sweet blessing,
And gain at last—so eagerly we sought—
Fear in possessing,

Unknowing, we,
The Hand that opes the door and bids us come,
Will keep us safe from harm till we shall see
Our far-off home!

THE OLD SOLDIER.

THOU hast passed through battles bloody,
Thou hast trod ensanguined fields,
And hast proved the world-wide proverb,
That a Briton never yields.
More than twenty years a soldier!
Thou art old and crippled now,
And the mark of many conflicts
Is cut deep upon thy brow.
Where was got that mark of bullet?
Where that sabre cut received?
Ah! those scars have won thee honor,

And from service thee relieved!
Dost regret it, war-won veteran?
Would'st yet mingle in the fray,
Where the sabres brightly glisten,
And the prancing chargers neigh?
Take the rest thy country gives thee,
Bravely hast thou served and well!
Sit thee down upon my hearthstone,
Of thy battles boldly tell.
How thou fought'st at Russia's stronghold,
Sieged Sebastopol's stout walls;
How upon the heights of Alma
Poured the shell and cannon balls.
Inkerman and Balaklava!
Names that thrill thy blood e'en yet,
With remembrance of the carnage
That thou never canst forget.
India's battles! ah, recount them!
I could listen to the theme
Till the night begins to broaden
Into daylight's wintry beam.
Rest then, soldier, old and hoary!
Rest, and drink, and eat thy fill.
Tell the tales of battle's glory,
With thy voice my pulses thrill!
Rest thee with thy country's blessing,
While thy comrades interpose,
As a wall of rock, their bodies
'Twixt the nation and its foes.
Rest thee! Take thy peace and comfort,
Thou hast done thy duty well;
How thou fought'st and bled'st for glory,
Future history shall tell!

GOOD NIGHT.

Written to close a S. of T. Open Division.

Good night ! good night ! the stars in heaven are shining,
The wind sighs fitfully about the eaves ;
The summer roses on the wall once climbing,
Drop to the earth their sere and dying leaves.

We meet in joy, though all around are saying
That summer's glory crowns rich autumn's head ;
The flowers she planted with such care and tended,
Are changed to fruit and woven with leaflets red.

Her toil is o'er ! another claims her treasure,
Enjoys, and leaves the dregs to be sipped up
By winter's withered lip, and woful pleasure,
Drank from the old man's care-embittered cup.

Even so with life ; in morning hours we labor
For that which we cannot enjoy or keep,
Laying up wealth which afterwards may vex us,
But will not satisfy our longings deep.

But there are riches which the heart may gather,
Which comfort us in age as well as youth ;
Treasures and toils that will reward us ever—
'Tis the pursuit of temperance and truth.

The incense of good deeds ' 'twill rise to heaven
When prayers and tears are counted no avail
When God's Archangel listens to the pleading
Of widowed wife or mournful orphan's wail.

The weak to strengthen, to uphold the erring,
To guide the soul aright in virtue's way,
To cast away the burning cup of pleasure,
And loose the inebriate from rum's dark sway.

To uphold our principles and Order ever!
Be not ashamed of our God-given work,
Join hand in hand, and heart from heart ne'er sever,
These are our duties, and we never shirk.

We've called you here, my friends, to give us courage,
To help us in the task we've undertaken,
To show you that our influence still is striving,
Our faith in temperance principles unshaken.

God bless you all! we ask your kindest wishes,
To help us in the path of truth and right;
We thank you for the kind attention shown us,
And bid yon each and all a kind good night!

THE RED RIBBON TIE.

The First "Ribbon" movement in Michigan was a Red Ribbon.

YOU may sing of the witchery that lies
In the roguish gleam of a pair of bright eyes;
Of the beauty that blooms on the maiden's cheek,
Of the loving thoughts that no tongue may speak;
But none of these can e'er compare,
Though boasting beauty rich and rare,
With the deep and lasting charms that lie
In the magical link of the Red Ribbon Tie.

A mother may sigh o'er a wayward son,
Whose feet so swiftly to ruin run,
As he sips of the cursed cup that's filled
With a drop of "damnation doubly distilled."
Till the head grows mad and the brain is dazed,
And the eyes once bright are dull and glazed,—
No charm can arrest his downward career,
Till a Red Ribbon Tie in his coat doth appear.

A wife may wail o'er a husband lost,
Of a hearth left lone, of a love oft crossed;
A sweetheart may plead, with a pretty pout,
That a lover on sprees too oft goes out;
A father may scold, a brother may talk
Of that son and brother's unsteady walk;
There's not half the persuasion that can lie
In the magical charm of the Red Ribbon Tie!

O, emblem blest, unpretending plain!
When a man his manhood would regain,
When he talks up the walk of life anew,
With a happy resolve his best to do;
With the help of God and his brother man,
He may rise to the level of virtue again,
If he only place in his buttonhole there
A Red Ribbon Tie, so fresh and fair!

Success to the badge! Success to the band!
Keep firm of heart, stand hand in hand!
Some day you'll triumph o'er ruin and rum!
Some day, indeed, shall the good time come,
When your flag shall float over valley and hill,
Over licensed hotel and illicit still,
And the monster drink shall bow his head
Through fear and shame of the Ribbon Red

MISCONCEPTION.

Is time unkind,
And memory but a jewel-hilted sword
That plucks my heart out with a tender word?
And thoughts of yesterday, a time of tears,
And hopes long vanished with the vanished years,
The years now old and gray?
And fancies, loves, and memories to-day
Troop in like ghosts, and stare from vacant eyes,
And laugh with fleshless lips, in mocking guise
Of those I loved and lost, and seek to bind
Their lives though lost to me?
Unkind, unkind!

If you could come,
And, holding both my hands in both your own,
Look in my eyes and say: "Time has not flown!
'Tis only we who have grown old and changed:
Our hearts which have become cold and estranged;
Time still is young and gay;
'Tis but imagination makes you say:
We once did love, we once were dearest friends,
'Tis but the glamour, youth and memory lends
To distant by-gone days, when fancy twined
Wreaths of forget-me-nots.
Time still is kind!"

Perhaps 'tis true!
In those old days, when love was new and sweet,
And every night but crowned the day complete;
And skies were sunnier, and flowers more fair,
Because my eyes but saw your image there;
And faith was firm and strong;

And neither night nor day was e'er too long;
For hope and happiness made all so bright
That memory of each was dear delight;
Then you swore love to me, but now you rue!
Time still is kind—
You only are untrue!

TEMPERANCE TOPICS.

WRITTEN IN 1870.

Mania a potu.

THERE was a youth, a bright-eyed glorious boy,
A favourite in the village where he dwelt,
A high-souled, genial, frank, engaging lad,
Whom everybody loved. The young obeyed,
The elders petted and caressed, and gave
A glass of wine or sherry, for he loved
Dearly the juice of the warm-glowing grape.
He grew to man's estate, and ever made
A leader in the circle where he moved.
He took himself a wife, the brightest there;
But she, who often proffered wine, with smiles,
Soon learned to dread the goblet as her death.
Her noble husband often drained the bowl,
Yea, filled and drained again, and oft again!
Till sense and reason fled, and he lay stretched,
A loathsome object at her dainty feet.
Yet this was but a vice occasional.
" A glass of wine hurts no man," he would say;
" A social glass or two with merry friends,
Makes time pass pleasantly;" and so again,
The next feast found him ready as before.

Pass twenty years and see him once again,
He lies upon a wretched bed of pain,
Goblins and ghouls, and serpents haunt his rest,
And everything a maddened brain can see
Is gloating over him with hellish glee.
Hear his mad voice and learn a lesson then—
Where he is, all may be, who shun not that
Which makes a brute of proud humanity.

"They have chained me here to my bed!
They have circled my bursting head
With an iron band so strong!
They have pinioned my hands, my feet,
And my heart has ceased to beat,
I have lain here so long.

"They think that I am dead,
They think that from me are fled
Reason, and sense, and life;
They've bereft me of all I prize,—
The light of my children's eyes,
The sunny face of my wife.

"The sunny face, did I say?
I saw the smile fade each day,
The shadow deepen and darken.
Could I once more hear her voice,
That so oft made my heart rejoice,
For my life I would hear and hearken.

"They tell me I did not know,
That I caused her tears to flow,
With my speech and ways insane;
But I knew ere it came to this,
I had robbed her life of bliss,
I had made it a barren bane.

"'Twas the poisonous fire that flowed
Through my veins, till my heart's blood glowed
In my puffed and swollen cheek;
'Twas damnation doubly distilled,
That my pulses and being filled,
Till my tongue refused to speak!

"It should have been dumb with sighs,
For it dimmed Mary's beautiful eyes,
And drove the smiles from her mouth;
I saw her grow old with pain,
But the poison that filled my brain
Was a mighty and terrible drouth,

"That dried up the springs of my love,
That drove me from things above
To grovelling in the mire;
That threw o'er my spirit a spell,
That gave me such visions of hell,
And devils dancing in fire.

"Just this moment I saw one stand,
Clutching a knife in one hand,
The other outstretched to me;
In vain do I writhe and cry;
What fires flash from his eye,—
There! see him turn and flee!

"I am not mad, but sick
With the sulphurous smoke, so thick
That it fills up the air of the room.
O, open some window or door!
See the serpents that crawl o'er the floor!
See the flashes that light up the gloom!

"Will not someone give me a knife?
I must even defend my life,—
Nay, indeed, I am not mad!
Who plays with such solemn grace?
Ah, that is my mother's face,
So holy, so sweet, so sad!

"O, mother, go back to your grave!
But why did not the rich man crave
For brandy, or even beer?
'Twould be easier sent to hell
Than water,—and tastes as well,
Nay, better than it does here!

"Give me a drop to drink!—
I will not take it, I think,
You have poison put in the cup!
Maddening fire without, within!
Ah, what horrid howling and din
Those fiends are keeping up!"

He ceased, and suddenly an ashen hue
Crept over his worn cheek; the light grew dim,
Flickered, and flared, and altogether died
From his once glorious eyes. He lies with those
Whose lamps have been in utter darkness quenched.

O, men of mighty minds, arise! stand forth!
Stretch out strong hands, and drive this cruel curse,
And all the want and misery it entails,
Off from the face of God's most glorious land!

www.ingramcontent.com/pod-product-compliance
Lightning Source LLC
Chambersburg PA
CBHW020800020726
47495CB00008B/2528
9783744773041